The
Saloon Girl's
Journey

Angela Castillo

To anyone who has ever
doubted your purpose.
God holds your destiny
In His careful hands.

Author's Note

As the nineteenth century came to a close in
Texas, the years were most tumultuous. Racial
issues reared their ugly heads, as they still do.
I have done my best to explore the time period
with an accurate voice, while trying to give
the utmost respect to the culture groups represented
in my story. So while the words I have chosen
might not always be politically correct, they
are historically correct, and I have attempted
to focus on positivity as much as possible.

ANGELA CASTILLO

Part One:
Sanctuary

1

A Place for Darla

DOWNS HOUSE

A PLACE OF SANCTUARY

FOR UNFORTUNATE WOMEN

Darla glanced over the sign and turned to Brother Jenkins. "Is that what you think I am? An unfortunate woman?"

Brother Jenkins eyed her for a moment, lips twitching under his sharp nose. "Er..."

He's staring at my eye. Darla reached up to touch the puffy area underneath. Though it had been healing for over a week, there'd still been a light greenish-purple bruise when she'd looked in the boarding house mirror that morning. Bruises still dotted her neck and arm, though the modest gown she'd been given by the church folks did a good job of covering them.

Her shoulders sagged as she glanced back down the road. "I suppose I've had a bit of bad luck. But things could have been worse, right? Hal never caught up with us out on the trail. We made it here safe and sound. All those are lucky things. I'd venture to say downright fortunate, wouldn't you?"

Brother Jenkins retrieved her carpet bag from the small cart and rubbed his chin. "Well, the hand of the Almighty intervened in a timely fashion. I cannot deny that."

"You bet He did." Darla squinted at the sign again. "Since I have nowhere else to go, I'll give the place a shot. But I ain't looking for any handouts."

"You will not be getting any handouts here." The pastor tied the horse's reins to a fence post. "Mrs. Downs doesn't put up with an ounce of laziness. You'll be expected to earn your keep, just like the rest of the women."

She tossed her head. "Well, that suits me just fine. I can work a mule into the ground and still have the strength to dance a jig on a table."

Two red spots bloomed on Brother Jenkins's cheeks. "Please don't do that."

Darla giggled and patted a few unruly blond curls back into place under her battered straw bonnet. "Sugar, it's just an expression."

He sighed. "I've been meaning to address your manner of speech. I realize these abrupt changes are hard for you, but you must temper these brazen habits of yours. Don't say 'ain't.' Don't treat people with such familiarity. Show some respect. Proper ladies don't talk like that."

Darla suppressed an eye-roll. The man was forever pointing out what proper ladies did and didn't do. "I don't much care about being dignified, but I'd like to become a better Christian."

The pastor's lips flattened out into a frown. "Yes, I know you made the decision to give your life to the Lord back there on the trail. It's more than a prayer, Darla. Do you understand the changes you must make in your life?"

Soonie was the most Christian person I've ever met, and she wasn't always proper. Despite the thought, Darla nodded. "Yes, I'm more certain than I've ever been about anything."

A rare smile spread across the pastor's pinched face. "I am glad, Darla. And I believe this will be the perfect place. But only if you follow the words of Christ and 'go and sin no more.'"

"If you mean flirtin' and dancin' and drinkin' then you've got nothing to worry about, Brother Jenkins. Saloons are rat traps and I have no intention of going back among the varmits. I'll do my very best."

"Seek God, and He will guide you. Now we'd better get inside, it's almost dark." Brother Jenkins swung open the imposing iron gate and waved Darla inside.

Skeletons of oaks and elms, bereft of finery for the cold season, held up trembling limbs to the gray sky. Darla and Brother Jenkins followed a path paved with flat stones, which led to the wide steps of a large home.

Columns of brickwork told of past grandeur, but paint peeled from the trim and in several places, boards had cracked and split. Even with these blemishes, the house had an air of dignity about it.

Brother Jenkins removed his black, wide-brimmed minister's hat and with spindly fingers, lifted the brass door knocker.

Darla bit her lip and stared at the door. Despite her brave words to Brother Jenkins, part of her wanted to pick up her skirts and run back down the road the way they had come. *What if these folks find out about my past? Brother Jenkins couldn't have told them the whole story. They wouldn't have agreed to keep me. Even this sort of place has limits on who they'll let in.* The question of how much Brother Jenkins had revealed burned in her mind but she couldn't bring herself to ask. Nothing to do but wait for a polite rejection and see what other place Brother Jenkins could rustle up. *Probably the poorhouse.* Never in all her days, even scantily clad before a room full of men, had she felt so anxious and exposed.

The door swung open, and a tall woman looked down at them. Darla's heart sank further. The lady was swathed in black, from the end of the ragged ostrich plume that graced her bonnet to the toes of the sensible shoes peeping from under her inky dress.

Brother Jenkins, who was rather tall himself, tipped back his head to meet her gaze. "Good evening. Mrs. Downs, I presume?"

"You presume much, for there are presently eight ladies living at this establishment, if you count the cook's daughter, and I do," said the woman. A stiff ribbon peeped from under her chin like a giant moth. "But yes, I am Mrs. Downs. The ladies call me Ma Downs. Hardly proper, but certain concessions must be made, mustn't they? I assume you've had your supper?"

The pastor blinked and nodded. "Yes, ma'am."

"Then we shall have a cup of tea." She led them into the narrow hallway, making a point to wipe her feet though she hadn't stepped an inch out the door, and glared at them beneath thick eyebrows until they followed suit.

Darla tried to wipe her shoes, but the white leather had been utterly devastated in the last week's adventures. *I can't very well remove my shoes.* She tugged on her skirts to try to cover her feet and hoped Ma Downs wouldn't notice the dreadful state of her footwear.

"You may place your things there." Ma Downs waved at an ornate bench set against the wall. The golden wood looked out of place against the drab purple wallpaper.

"That is a goodly piece of furniture," Brother Jenkins remarked.

"Yes. My son, Ethan, made it. He is a great help to me." Ma Downs made a sharp turn through a door to the right.

Any bit of dusky light that might have found its way into the room was trapped in thick muslin drapes hanging over the windows. The furniture was old and overstuffed, all covered with the same gold and black patterned material. An organ sat in the corner. Ma Downs indicated a chair and Darla perched on the edge of it, trying not to jiggle her knees.

"I'll return in a moment." Ma Downs swept out of the room like an enormous crow, skirts swirling around her like ruffled feathers.

Brother Jenkins tapped his chin with the brim of his hat.

"Do you think she'll let me stay?" Darla whispered.

His eyebrows shot up, and he put a finger to his lips.

Ma Downs came back into the room, a tray with a porcelain teapot and cups cradled in her hands. "Here we are." She set the tray on a small table, poured the tea and handed steaming cups to Brother Jenkins and Darla.

"Now." She settled into a chair opposite from Darla. "The pastor's telegram said your name is Darla North. You grew up in an orphanage, and later worked in various professions. Is that correct?"

"Yes ma'am. Anything you could think of. Some I ain't . . . I'm mean, I'm not so proud of." Darla darted a glance at Brother Jenkins, but he stared into his cup, drinking in slow, careful sips.

"Of course." The woman peered at her through tiny spectacles, ludicrous on her wide, flat face. Her eyes lingered on Darla's bruised eye. "You will find that our girls come from all kinds of places and have done all sorts of jobs. We care nothing for the past."

Even saloon girls? I doubt you'd have let me cross that bright and shiny welcome mat if you knew I'd worked in dens of iniquity, or whatever Brother Jenkins called them.

"As long as a person does the work expected of them here, abides by the rules, and lives a scrupulous life of morality, she can stay under our roof." Ma Downs continued. "Stray off the path, and she will be asked to leave."

"I'll do my best, ma'am." Darla sat up a little straighter and smoothed her skirt. The old windows rattled with a brisk December wind. A tiny sigh escaped her lips. *Perhaps I won't be turned out . . . tonight, anyway.*

"I can attest Miss North is a hard worker," said Brother Jenkins. "I believe she will do her best to fit in and do what is asked of her."

"I'm glad to have your assurance, but we do have a trial period for every woman who stays here."

A trial period? Darla tightened her grip around the frail china cup, paying no mind to the porcelain burning her skin. *I wonder how long? Or is it different for everyone?* She was too afraid to ask.

"I'm sure she'll do fine," Brother Jenkins replied, but he gave Darla a slanted look.

"Then it's settled." Mrs. Downs stood and gathered the tea cups, including Darla's half full one, back on the tray. She leaned into the hall. "Lisbeth," she called. "Please come here."

Feet padded down the stairs, and a girl appeared in the doorway. Tall and willowy, she seemed near Darla's age, in her early twenties.

Mrs. Downs beckoned her into the room. "Lisbeth, this is Darla. Will you please show her where she'll be staying?"

The girl swept a thick curtain of pale red hair back from her face and nodded.

Darla stood and held her hand out to Brother Jenkins. "Thank you so much . . . for everything."

"I'll pray for you, Darla." His steely eyes sent her another message. A plea to behave herself. To not make him regret his recommendation. Then his eyes softened, and he shook her hand. "Yes, I'll be praying."

Darla gave him what she hoped was a reassuring smile. "I'll make you glad you brought me, sug--sir. I promise." She moved into the hallway and picked up her carpet bag. After fumbling around for a moment, she pulled out her small pistol and the tiny dagger she had kept with her at all times in the saloon. "Here. Please take these. You'll need them more than I will, in your travels."

"The Lord is my strength and shield. But you'll do well to be rid of them." He put the items in his pocket.

Ma Downs, who had witnessed the exchange, nodded. "There is no need for such things in this house." She opened the door for Brother Jenkins, and followed him outside.

Darla stood in the hall, wondering if she should run after him for last minute instructions, but Lisbeth plucked at her arm. "Come on. You can bring your things."

The stairs creaked under Darla's filthy shoes as she followed Lisbeth. Steep, narrow, and ending in shadows, they reminded her of the staircase at the saloon. But the upper story had always been a welcome refuge at the end of the day. No man was allowed to put a boot past the first step. It was a relief every night to move up the stairs and away from the dirty, brawling men, who took liberties and stole kisses and relentlessly demanded drinks and dances.

But I won't be coming back down to that world, she reminded herself. *Now I serve a different master, a God who loves me, even though He knows everything I've done.*

Lisbeth reached the top and started down a long hallway with rows of doors lined up on either side like sentries. She turned the knob of the third door on the left. "You will share a room with me. I hope that's all right." Her voice was lilting and soft.

Why, she's Irish! Darla had only met one other person from Ireland; a farmhand who'd briefly worked for her dad when she was a child.

"Of course I don't mind. I've slept on the ground a few times in the last week, so I'm just thankful for a real bed." Darla followed Lisbeth into the room.

During the interview, night had fallen. Moonlight filtered into the room through lace curtains, as dainty and pretty as the drapes downstairs had been dull and dreary. Twisted bits of wood and rocks of various shapes and colors had been placed on the window sill. Two beds on either side of the window were covered in cheery quilts.

Darla touched the bright fabric. "Why is everything so lovely up here, while the rooms downstairs are drab and dowdy? Besides that beautiful bench in the entry way, I mean."

Lisbeth shrugged. "Unfortunates should spend their time pondering the ways of God," she chanted, as though reading from a book. "They should turn away from worldly vanities and think on heavenly things."

"Is that what Ma Downs says?" asked Darla.

"No, but the benefactors believe it. Since they supply most of the funds for the house and other works we do, Ma Downs tries to keep them happy. So downstairs is shabby. But we are allowed to keep our rooms the way we like, within reason. The benefactors never come up here."

"If Heaven looks like the parlor downstairs, I'm not sure if I want to go." Darla glanced up to see if Lisbeth was shocked.

A ghost of a smile crept across the girl's pale lips. "I don't know if I would either. I figure, if God made sunsets and butterflies, he must like colors just fine." She gestured to a bureau. "You can put your belongings in the two lower drawers. The wash basin is over by the window if you'd like to freshen up before lights out."

"Thank you." Darla pulled a drawer open and placed her few things inside, wishing she could have gotten rid of the scandalous lace petticoats left from her saloon days. So far, she hadn't been able to purchase anything else. *I can't very well go without under things.*

If Lisbeth was scandalized by the clothes, she didn't say anything about them. "I'll be back in a few minutes," she said, and closed the door in her wake.

Darla washed her face and hands, removed the horrid shoes and cleaned her feet with a soft cloth hanging on a hook beside the basin. She changed into a nightdress and peeked out the window to the yard below.

The grounds were bathed in moonlight. On the left sat a courtyard and the front gate, and to her right the property stretched out into pasture, with a barn and gardens. A small gazebo caught her attention. *Could the son have built that too?*

She closed the shutters, almost slamming her finger. "Dratted window," she muttered, then covered her mouth and looked around. She doubted that 'dratted' was an acceptable word in this home.

How am I going to do this? Darla sank down on the quilt and ran her fingers along the even threaded lines. Every stitch had its place. *Can I possibly fit in here?*

Lisbeth came back in, settled in her chair, and began to work on a bit of embroidery.

"Your needlework is beautiful." Darla admired the knotted flowers covering the thick white cloth.

"Mountmellick," came the reply.

"Oh. An Irish technique?"

"Yes." Lisbeth lowered her head.

Darla gave up on the conversation. Some of the other saloon girls had been quiet like Lisbeth. *She might be shy. I'll give her some time.*

After flipping to a random page in the Bible Pastor Jenkins had given her, Darla read a passage in a book called Lamentations. Even after reading the chapter through twice, she couldn't make a lick of sense out of it. Everyone was sad, that's all she could figure. Flipping to a different section, a verse in Galatians caught her eye.

"But the fruit of the Spirit is love, joy, peace, longsuffering, gentleness, goodness, faith, meekness, temperance: against such there is no law."

Longsuffering. Doesn't that mean patience? She tapped her fingers against her head, trying to remember long-ago Sunday school lessons. Finally she closed her Bible, turned down the quilt, and got into bed.

She had to stifle a squeal of excitement as her toes slid all the way down to the end of the sheets. *What luxury after the crazy places I've slept in the last few days.* Her hair spilled out over the pillow, brushed and free of tangles. Looping a curl around her finger, she smiled.

"Well, goodnight," said Lisbeth as she crossed the room and blew out the lantern.

"Lisbeth?" said Darla as she heard the girl settle into the bed across from her.

"Yes, Darla?"

"How long is the testing time? Until I know if I'll get to stay?"

Lisbeth's bed creaked as she rolled over to face the wall. "It's different for everyone. But you'll know."

"How?"

Quiet, steady breathing was the only answer.

If only I could find rest as quickly. When Darla closed her eyes, faces flickered before her. Girls from the business she had left behind, battered and tired under the bright paint. Faces of the Comanche and Kiowa people who lived in the settlement where she'd stayed for a few days after her escape from the Easy Dipper Saloon. And an evil man named Hal who'd uprooted those people and scattered them to the winds. Including her friend, a part-Comanche girl named Soonie.

Where is Soonie? I'll probably never see her again. But she'll be all right. Soonie had a strong young man. They would take care of each other.

She clutched her pillow, waiting for sleep. *This seems like a good place to be. If only I can make it through the trial period.*

2

Meeting Ethan

*D*arla woke with a desire to explore the grounds out back. *Especially the little gazebo.* It had been a long time since she'd been on anything resembling a farm, and she wanted to find out more about her new home.

Lisbeth's bed was already empty and the covers pulled smooth. Darla wasn't surprised she'd been left to sleep; the girl had said new members of the house were always given a day to get used to the order of things before they were asked to help.

Draped over a corner armchair were clothes provided by the charity. Darla spread the dress over her arm and pursed her lips. Large swirls that looked like pink cabbage heads covered the fabric. *It's ugly as pig snouts, and far too big.* However, it would keep her warm during outside chores. She put on the horrible dress and found a bright green sash in her drawer to cinch it around her waist. *I had much worse at the orphanage.*

Venturing down the stairs, she listened for voices or signs of activity. Silence met her ears. *Should I try to find someone?* She crept to the door. *I'll just take a peek at the gardens before anyone sees me. What could it possibly hurt?*

A worn path led around the house and past a workshop. A hammering sound echoed through the wall.

She went on through a smaller gate and into an enclosed area, which she assumed would host a garden in the spring. And there was the gazebo.

Five posts supported the structure, each of them covered in delicately carved hummingbirds, doves and other birds of flight. Darla stepped into the small structure to examine the inside more closely. The roof dripped with curlicues and vines. Suspended from the center of the ceiling, a carved cherub held a trumpet so realistic it seemed as though musical notes would play at any moment.

Darla sank onto one of the wooden benches. Peace washed over her, and she closed her eyes and listened as winter birds sang good mornings to each other.

Whatever is required of me at the house, I can handle it. But it'll be nice to come out here sometimes to have a break from that dreary parlor.

Ethan Downs slid the plane across the glossy red wood. A few slivers curled beneath the blade, fine as angel hairs. He ran his hand over the surface.

Smooth as silk, and such a nice color. Too bad I have to use it to repair that floor joist. As long as he could remember, wood had spoken to him, told him what to make from it. And this longleaf pine plank begged to be something beautiful--part of a baby's cradle maybe, or a corner shelf in some fancy sitting room.

"You'll have to accept your fate, same as all of us," he told the board, then chuckled. *People would think I'm crazy, talking to a piece of wood.* Sometimes the mundane labor got to him, the menial tasks that must be done to keep the ancestral home standing. But if he didn't do it, who would? He shook his head. Ethan didn't resent being a part of the ministry carried on by his family for generations. But all the time wasted on repairs could have been spent making much more beautiful things.

Picking up a thumb-sized scrap off the floor, he started to whittle. In a few moments, a half-bloomed rose began to form in the soft wood.

"That's pretty."

Ethan almost dropped his creation. He turned to see the silhouette of a girl in the barn door, bathed in the golden light of dawn.

She stepped inside.

Perhaps twenty, the girl's eyes had a wild, scattered look, as though they held tales of things best not spoken aloud. A smile twisted up in the corner of lips almost too red to be natural, and wisps of bright blond hair curled beneath a shabby straw bonnet. Her frock and apron hung loose on her shoulders, as though they had been made for someone else. *Ma must've given her something from the mission barrel.* His mother was forever trying to help the ladies develop character and purge worldly vanities. *It's not going to work for this one. She'd look pretty in a gunny sack.*

The girl laughed. "Well, are you just gonna stand there and let flies take up housekeeping in your mouth, or can you say hello?" She put one hand on her hip, and held the other toward him. "I'm Darla North, and I'd like to make your acquaintance."

"Uh, hello." Ethan offered his hand with the rose still in it, stared at the carving and shoved it in his pocket. He opened his palm once more. "Ethan Downs. Ma told me you came in last night."

"So Ma Downs truly is your ma?" The smile curved up once more, but nothing in her expression or tone suggested mockery, only good fun. She shook his hand firmly. "Yep, I got dragged in by the cat, I guess. Or traveling preacher. Whichever you'd prefer. Do you live here?"

How did she *end up at Down's House?* The shed seemed transformed by sudden light and color.

Though both of them wore clothes barely more than rags, Ethan felt as though they should be at some fancier place, like a county dance.

"Um, yes." He gathered himself, remembering she had just asked him a question. "My father died three years ago, and my brother left to join the Texas Rangers, so I help look after things. I have a little place at the back of the property."

"Oh, I see." Darla trailed a slender finger across the board he'd been finishing. "I visited the gazebo. Did you make it?"

"Yes. I build things. Some stay here, and some I sell, to help pay the bills." Ethan pulled the rose out of his pocket and twirled it in his hands. "I don't get much time to carve trinkets. If I didn't fix things, the house would fall down around our ears."

"How many . . . what do you call us . . . unfortunates live here?" Darla walked to the doorway and turned her back to him, clasping her hands behind her.

"Hey now, I didn't come up with the name. But there's six ladies right now, including yourself. There's room for a dozen." Ethan couldn't tear his eyes away from the girl's hair, which shone like molten gold in the morning light. None of the other ladies ever had hair like that.

Over Darla's shoulder he saw a billowing shape come through the front door of the house and stand on the porch. "Ethan!" his mother called. "Ethan, will you please come here?"

"I'd better see what she needs. And it's almost time for breakfast." Ethan jerked his head in the direction of the house. "Our cook, Mrs. Betty, usually doesn't have much to work with, but she could make old burlap taste good." He stepped up to pass Darla.

She laid a hand on his arm, "May I have it?" she asked.

"Have what?" Heat rose to his face. *Ethan Downs, pull yourself together. She's just a girl . . . and probably been through a world of hurt, just like everyone else.* He swallowed a lump in his throat and forced his lips back into a smile.

"May I have the rose? It's so pretty, and it didn't take you long to make."

He held it up to the light. "Give me a little more time, and I'll make it even better."

"All right." She gave him a full smile, and a single dimple flashed on her right cheek. "You ain't . . . I mean aren't . . . going to forget, are you?"

"Of course I won't forget." He watched her step out the door, skirts swishing. She'd disappeared by the time he realized he hadn't asked her a single thing about herself.

###

"I would rather you ask me before traipsing out in the yards on your own so early in the morning." Ma Downs's ostrich plumes, already in place, shook with each word.

Darla nodded, her heart pounding in her ears. When she had seen Ma Downs's frown, she thought she might be turned out right then. It was going to take some time to get used to this new home and the rules set before her. *But I've got nowhere else to go. I've got to learn how to act if I want to be fit for a better place than a saloon.*

A sudden warmth crept over her, and she remembered the verse she'd read the night before about the fruits of the Spirit. *Patience.* The word rose up, unbidden. *I've never been patient in my life. God is going to have to teach it to me.*

"So, are we agreed?" Ma Downs's eyes softened. "Poor girl. I can see you have been over some rough roads. We want you to do well here. But I must hold everyone to the same rules, otherwise . . ."

"Yes, Ma'am. I understand."

"Now let's go have breakfast; everyone else is already waiting."

Darla followed, the jumble of rules she'd been told so far jumping through her mind. *Don't leave the house without permission. Clothing must be approved by Ma Downs. Lights out by 9:00.What's next?* She shook her head. The only rules in the saloon were don't get caught stealing, never allow a patron's wife inside the building, and stay away from Mr. Gandro when he was drunk.

The same type of muslin curtains used in the parlor darkened the dining room. It was lit only by candles flickering from two rickety candelabras. A long table covered by a black cloth filled most of the room. Few other details could be seen in the dim light.

Three women were lined up behind chairs on the right side of the table and Lisbeth stood with one other lady on the left.

Ma Downs nodded to the empty chair beside Lisbeth. "You may sit there."

Darla scooted over and plopped down in the seat.

Lisbeth raised her eyebrows. Two of the other ladies tittered behind cloth napkins.

Darla glanced at everyone else. They were all still standing. She stood up quickly, and her chair crashed to the floor.

Ethan emerged from the table's shadowy end, rushed over and righted the offending seat before she could reach it. Wordlessly, he returned to his place.

Ma Downs's lips remained in the same tight line during these proceedings. When Ethan was settled she finally spoke. "Are we quite ready, then?"

Darla fought the urge to crawl under the table. "Yes," she managed to squeak.

Ma Downs bowed her head. "Lord, we thank Thee for your many provisions . . ."

A very long prayer followed which seemed to address the ailments of every citizen in Dallas and perhaps a few outside of the city as well.

Darla's stomach growled loudly, and one of the girls across the table giggled again. Darla didn't blame her. *Never in all my born days have I felt like such a clumsy oaf.*

When she opened her eyes, Ethan flashed her a sympathetic smile.

At least I have one friend here. But I bet he'd never speak to me again if he knew who I used to be.

3

Cows and Conversation

The next]morning, Darla's slumber was interrupted by a voice calling her name. When her eyes fluttered open, Lisbeth's white face floated above her.

"Milking time," the Irish girl said.

When Lisbeth stepped back, Darla thought she saw something furry crawl down the thin shoulder, half hidden by hair.

Darla scooted back in her bed. "What was that? On your arm?"

Lisbeth blinked. "Nothing. Nothing at all."

A fuzzy face peeked out between the long, red strands and chittered at Darla.

"A squirrel! What a darling little thing. Is he yours?"

Lisbeth's cheeks reddened. "Yes, his name is Danny, after my grandfather. I rescued him from a cat when he was a baby. But please don't tell Ma Downs, all right? She can't abide rodents and I know she'd make me let him go. And he needs me." She stroked the little animal's head with a slender finger. "Don't you, Danny?"

Danny grabbed her finger in his paws.

"Don't worry, I won't tell." Darla climbed out of bed. "Does he stay up here during the day?"

"I have a box for him. No one else comes in here. The ladies are expected to keep their own rooms clean."

"That's lucky." Darla had decided to play a little game with herself, which involved pointing out whenever something was fortunate, since everyone here was so convinced of the opposite.

She turned bleary eyes towards the window, but no morning light welcomed her.

"What time is it anyway?" she asked Lisbeth, who was already dressed.

"Half-past five. So we're late today. I let you sleep in a bit, so hurry up."

"Sleep in?" Darla yawned. Due to late nights at the saloon, she normally wouldn't be awake until the sun was high in the sky. *Lisbeth must think I'm a complete sloth for sleeping so late yesterday.*

With fumbling fingers, she buttoned her dress and shuffled down the stairs after her roommate.

The barn stood at the edge of the pasture, dilapidated but stately, like most of the other buildings on the property. Various farm implements rusted in the tall grass, abandoned, as new and better devices had come along. *Or perhaps they planted large crops at one time, but no longer have the workers to care for acres of land.*

Several cows mooed as the girls entered the building. The sweet scent of hay mixed with pungent manure instantly transported Darla to her childhood. She'd always

26

been awake this early on the farm, following her father and helping with his work.

"The supplies are in here." Lisbeth opened a side stall and handed her a clean pail and cloth. "Water for cleaning should be on the shelf by the cows already, Ethan usually fills it for us when he feeds the animals." She looked over at Darla. "I'm going to tidy up in here a bit. Can you manage alone?"

"I think so." Darla carried the items into the large open half of the barn, where five cows had been lined up and tied to posts. After moistening her cloth in the bucket of water, she approached the first cow, a large black and white animal that mooed at her approach.

"I'm a stranger, but I'll do my best," she said to the cow. Words her father had spoken years ago when he'd first taught her the task flooded back into her mind. *Clean the udder with the cloth. Place your stool in just the right spot so the cows can't kick you or the pail. Don't pull too hard or too soft, or all you'll get is a cantankerous cow.* She inhaled sharply and closed her eyes. It had been so long since she'd allowed herself to think about her dad's voice. She wiped a tear away on her sleeve and concentrated on her chore.

Thin streams of milk landed in the bucket with a satisfying hiss.

A throat cleared behind her.

Darla craned her neck to see Ethan standing in the doorway. He wasn't wearing a hat, and thick brown curls stood out from his head with wooly abandon, not slicked back like they had been at meals in the house.

"Good morning." He strode over and grabbed the cow's tail, which had been switching closer and closer to the pail.

"Thank you. Good morning." Heat rose to Darla's cheeks and she concentrated on the milk going into the bucket. *Land sakes. It's not like I've never seen a man before.*

"Did you sleep good? I know the rooms here aren't fancy."

"It's fine for me. Thank you. I'm glad I'm not riding a horse across the wilds right now."

"Yeah? Is that what you usually do?" His eyes were wide and interested.

"Well, not all the time. But the last week or so." Darla lowered her head and hoped he wouldn't ask any dangerous questions.

"I like riding. It helps me sort out my thoughts."

She looked over at him. "I know what you mean. But not when you're being chased by someone who wants to shoot you dead."

"No joshing?" Ethan dropped the cow's tail and stared at her. "Who'd want to hurt a sweet girl like you?"

Darla draped her cloth over her knee. "I don't feel like talking about it just yet. I'm sorry."

"Not to worry." Ethan lowered his eyes. "Maybe some other time." The cow's tail moved again, and he grabbed the end right before it slapped her face. "I came in to ask you something. Every day we take a big pot of soup around town in a wagon to the sick and elderly," he said. "Would you like to come with me this afternoon? It'll allow you to meet some of the folks we help and show you part of our mission here at Downs House."

Darla stood, picked up the bucket and poured it in the large jug by the wall. "I'm at your service, Mr. Downs."

"Everyone calls me Ethan." He picked up the large collecting jug and hoisted it into the next stall. "And I'm not forcing you to come." He studied her with grey-green eyes. "I just thought you might want to see the town and get out of the house."

"Sounds nice." Darla rinsed the cloth and rung it out. "Let me know when I should be ready."

"After breakfast." Ethan disappeared through the barn door.

Lisbeth came in from the side room, swinging an extra milk bucket. "I see you've met the man of the place."

"Yes. We met last night, actually." Darla turned so Lisbeth wouldn't see her flushed cheeks. "He seems nice enough."

Lisbeth put the pail down and twisted a section of hair around her finger. "He is . . . but don't be getting any ideas. He hasn't had a sweetheart for a long time."

Darla's head snapped up. "I declare, Lisbeth, I had no particular notions! But I wonder why he ain't . . . isn't married? Or engaged? Is his ma too smothering?"

Lisbeth shrugged. "I guess it's probably because of Sarah, his fiancée. They were going to get married, but she skipped town right before the wedding. Her family told Ethan she didn't wish to speak to him again, and no one ever found out why."

"How sad." *How could a woman be cruel to Ethan? He seems so kind. And he sure ain't . . . isn't hard on the eyes.* Dust from the barn settled on Darla's skin and made her feel as though she was wearing a powdery mask. She wiped her face with her apron. "When did all that happen?"

"About two years ago. And then Lew, Ethan's older brother, left. So Ethan stuck around to help out." Lisbeth frowned. "Of course, that was right before I came to live here. I heard about it from some of the other ladies."

"Do ladies come and go often?"

Lisbeth poured her milk in the large pail. "Some find husbands and get married, and Ma Downs is always checking the newspaper for employment suitable for one of us. But some stay longer than others. Indigo has been here the longest."

Darla leaned against the barn wall. "So I could be sent away to . . . I don't know, work in a factory?"

"No one's going to a factory." Lisbeth rolled her eyes. "Ma Downs would never force a woman to go somewhere she doesn't want to be."

"Well, that's fortunate." Darla's stomach grumbled. "Is it breakfast time yet?"

Lisbeth laughed. "I'm hungry too. They should be ringing the bell any time now. No one goes with an empty belly. We get rooms to lay our heads and a chance to keep our souls. Not many other places in this world where women like us could do that."

The pale blue eyes pierced into Darla's heart, and for a startling instant she wondered if Lisbeth had some sort of second sight, to see into the secrets of her past.

What an absurd notion. She shrugged and followed the girl through the door.

At breakfast, a little black girl Darla hadn't seen before darted around the table delivering platters of bacon and steaming biscuits. Her hair, like dark cotton, was gathered in a bun at the nape of her neck and her apron was fashioned from bright scraps of fabric.

"Who is that?" Darla whispered to Lisbeth while Ma Downs was looking the other way.

"Patience. She's the cook's daughter."

At home on Dad's farm, the hired hands and members of the house all ate at the same table. But, Darla remembered, they had all been white. People with different colored skin weren't allowed to eat at the same table, just like Comanches weren't allowed to live in the state of Texas. *Why does skin color play such a part in our customs? I wonder how God feels about that.*

Last night, she'd been far too flustered to pay much attention to the other women at the table, though Lisbeth had introduced her to everyone between meals. Today she studied everyone a bit closer while she ate her breakfast.

Indigo sat beside Lisbeth. She was thin and dark-haired, with a jagged scar that ran down the side of her face like a tear stain.

Sadie and Marnie Pennel sat on the other side of the table. They were sisters, a few years older than Darla. They seemed to giggle more than they talked.

At forty-ish, Mrs. Brodie was the oldest of "The Unfortunates" as Darla had begun to call them in her head. She was petite as a child and held her spoon in claw-like fingers, studying her eggs as though she suspected they might be poisoned.

Ma Downs surveyed everyone with a contented air, like a mother hen regarding her chicks.

Ethan smiled at her from his end of the table, and Darla dug a spoon into her bowl of grits, finding that she looked forward to the morning's errands with great anticipation.

Darla came down the front porch carrying loaves of bread wrapped in cloths. She smiled at Ethan, and his eyes lit up.

A different look flickered over Ma Downs's face. She squinted as she took the bread from Darla and placed it in the cart.

Darla knew that look. Mothers used to give it to her all the time during the saloon days when she'd winked at their sons on the street.

I can't help it if Ethan's taken a fancy to me, she huffed inside. *I don't rightly know how any man could think me attractive in these dowdy sacks she's given me to wear. Not that I'm ungrateful.* Wrapped up in these thoughts, she stepped squarely into a puddle. Mud splattered the leather shoes, which she'd worked so hard to clean the night before.

Darla looked back at Ma Downs and tried to smile. *These people have given me a place to stay and honest work,* she reminded herself. *I must do what I can to keep in their good graces. I've got no business flirting with this man, especially when he has been through so much pain.*

"Have a good day," Ma Downs told Ethan. Her eyes slanted back to Darla, resting on her face. "And please be careful. Looks like it won't rain, at least." The tall woman swished back into the house.

"Isn't that fortunate?" Darla called after her.

Ethan raised an eyebrow.

Darla tried adopting a more dignified stride back up to the porch to fetch the remaining bread, but only succeeded in slipping on the third stair.

Ethan caught her shoulder. "Whoa, there. You don't want to end up in the mud."

"I believe I've forgotten how to walk this morning." Darla managed to make it up the stairs and back again with the rest of the bread. She peered over the side of the small wooden cart. A giant cast-iron kettle squatted in the back, with a dipper hanging on the lip.

"No bowls?" she asked.

"Most people bring their own. You'll see." Ethan tightened the straps on the mule's halter. He tugged on the animal's lead and the cart trundled through the gate, down past the grand old houses of the neighborhood. Each was situated several hundred yards from the other, some separated by patches of trees and stately, tall fences. Many of the homes had been lovingly maintained, repainted and repaired. But a few seemed barely livable, with sagging porches and jagged, broken windows.

The tenth house was the worst of them, looking as though a sneeze might bring it crashing down. Ethan halted at the front gate and tied the mule's lead to a rotted fence post.

"He doesn't spook easily, does he?" Darla imagined the beast bolting, the gate clattering down the road behind him.

"Nope." Ethan rang a rusty bell by the gate.

The front door swung open. A woman who looked so frail that a brisk wind might blow her away came out and shuffled down the path. A man in similar condition soon came behind her. Bringing up the rear was a little dog. It bounded around their feet, ears perked and tail wagging.

Darla put a hand up to her mouth and silently prayed neither person would trip and fall to their deaths, but the couple and dog moved in perfect rhythm, like they had been doing the same dance for years.

The man and woman reached the cart and held out crudely carved bowls in withered hands.

"Mr. and Mrs. Wysmith, how are things?" Ethan ladled soup into the bowls and handed the woman a loaf of bread.

Mrs. Wysmith pursed her lips until they almost disappeared into wrinkles. "Oh, about how they should be, son. The winter breezes blow right through the parlor, you know, since the storm damaged the wall."

Ethan put a gentle hand on her shoulder. "I'll come by to take a look this afternoon. And I'll try to bring some firewood, if any can be spared."

"Bless you, son." The bright eyes, sunk deeply into aged sockets, studied Darla's face. "Now, who is this pretty girl you've brought along today?" Mrs. Wysmith grinned, revealing a mouth of rotten teeth.

"I'm Darla. Here, let me help you carry your bread." Darla took the loaf from the woman's shaking hands, worried it might end up in the mud.

Mrs. Wysmith leaned heavily on her arm as they headed back to the house, with Mr. Wysmith shuffling behind.

"That Ethan," Mrs. Wysmith said. "We've known the lad since he was a baby, and he'll have a special place in Heaven, sure is sure. We'd be starved and frozen to death if it weren't for the good folks livin' in the Downs."

"Not all of them have been good. You memberin' that Cathy Hale?" wheezed Mr. Wysmith, speaking for the first time. "She stole sumthin'. Must have been a spoon, weren't it, Mother?"

Mrs. Wysmith waved her hand, a movement perilous to her balance. "Yes, yes, but she didn't stay too long. Ma Downs don't hold with that kind of behavior."

The small party reached the front porch steps.

"I promise I won't take your spoons." Darla opened the door and placed the bread on the dingy counter inside. "You two have a lovely day now, you hear?" Before she could stop herself, she winked at the old man.

His eyes, which had been glittery slits for most of the conversation, popped open. "Did ya see that, Mother? That pretty gal winked at me!" A slow grin spread over his face. "I ain't had a woman wink at me in a coon's age."

Darla picked up her skirts and fled down the path. Her heart was pounding when she reached the cart.

Ethan gave her a lazy smile. "They're just elderly folks, not ghosts."

"Oh, I know. They were delightful. It's just . . . Oh, never mind." Darla fell back in step with the cart, wondering if she'd ever learn how to be a proper lady.

4

Tempting Tune

"I'm sorry, we don't have any more." Darla gave an apologetic smile.

The toothless woman holding a cracked earthen platter shot her a dark look and limped away without a word.

Darla dropped the ladle into the pot. "Poor thing. I know what it's like to go hungry. Could we go back to the house and fetch something for her?"

"Don't worry, she's from the poor farm." Ethan placed the lid over the container. "The city has a place where people can work for room and board. She'll get supper tonight."

"I'm glad." Darla squinted after the woman, who had almost reached the end of the street. *Is that where I would be if it weren't for the kindness of Ma Downs? The poor farm?* She shivered. It didn't sound like a very nice place.

Ethan tied the lead to a post. "Darla, would you mind waiting here for a moment?" He gestured to a side street. "I'd like to check on a man who lives down that way. This part of the street looks too muddy for the cart and I'd rather not have to dig it out of a rut. Besides, this fellow can be a bit crazy now and then." He rubbed his chin. "He gets kind of spooked around strangers."

Darla drew herself up. "You don't think I can handle crazy?"

"Well . . ." A hint of red tinged Ethan's cheeks. "He has been known to forget his clothes on occasion."

As if that would shock me. "All right, I suppose I can stand here and listen to the grass grow."

While Ethan disappeared down the muddy lane, a tune drifted through the winter breeze to Darla's ear. Tinny piano music held the promise of laughter and scalding beverages to chase away the cold and troubles of the world, if only for a little while. She turned to listen. She'd only worked at one saloon with a piano, and the instrument had been the establishment's only attribute. Sometimes when the place was closed, she'd go downstairs and attempt to pick out tunes on the cracked ivory keys.

I should stay here and wait for Ethan. Why go looking for trouble? But her fingers had other notions. In an instant she'd untied the lead and was pulling the mule in the direction of the familiar sound. Around one turn, and then another, until she found herself on a main city street.

"Ohhhh." Various jobs had led her through a string of one-horse towns. Nothing could have prepared her for the long rows of buildings set out on the lane. Fancy buggies and shabby carts jostled for a path down the cobblestones, and dozens of people strolled over the boardwalks. Some paused before shop windows to examine the latest wares being offered, while others hurried on mysterious errands, known only to themselves.

Darla ducked her head and guided the mule towards the music, until she stood before a gaudy building with a false front.

A wide, gleaming porch opened to the street. Hand-painted signs advertising the saloon's attractions covered the walls and posts.

DANCING GIRLS!

BEST WHISKEY IN DALLAS!

Darla couldn't see through the darkened windows, but men's laughter rang through the walls. A woman's voice, slightly off-key, sang along with the piano.

Her toes twitched in her shoes, and she fought the urge to step up and peek through the window. *How fancy are these Dallas saloons anyway?*

She folded her arms against herself. *I'm not going any closer. I'd better leave right now. Ethan will be wondering about me.*

"Hey, down there!" A lady wearing a fluffy silk dress that would have given Ma Downs a fit of vapors called from the balcony. "Did you lose your way, Goldilocks?"

Darla bit back a rude reply and shook her head. "No, just listening to the music, that's all."

The saloon girl descended a tiny spiral staircase, lifting high her already scandalously short skirts with a white-gloved hand. "I see." She tipped back the parasol she held and surveyed Darla with an appraising eye. "Yes, I had a feeling. You're one of them common girls. It's the way you walk. Ain't no hidin' it."

Darla's palms grew sweaty and she fought the urge to wipe them on the skirts of her dress. "I beg your pardon!"

"No sense getting uppity, ladies of entertainment can spot each other a mile off. Oughta know that, don't ya? Except I's got my morals and stipulations."

"Stipulations?" Darla's fingers crept to her cheeks. "Are you calling me a brothel girl? Because I'm not one of those. It was our job to keep men coming back for whiskey and dances, but that was all."

"My mistake, darlin'." The woman pulled a small pot of rouge from the recesses of her dress and rubbed a dot of color into each cheek. "Still . . ." She glanced back up at Darla, her gaze lingering on the bruised eye. "You look like you've had it kinda rough. Here the men treat us like gold. The owner wouldn't stand for us to be hurt. More 'n one time he's chased some brutish fellow down the street with a shotgun."

"That must be nice." Darla said in spite of her irritation. One especially awful night came to mind. She and two other girls had hidden in the stables during a saloon-wide brawl. Three men had died, and another girl had her arm broken when she'd been pushed down the front porch stairs.

The woman, whose eyes already bore tiny laugh lines, clicked her tongue. "You poor dear. Sometimes we don't have a choice about where we end up, do we?" She patted Darla's arm with plump fingers that sparkled with rings. "I'd suggest you come and ask for a job here, but my boss won't hire a common small-town girl, even if she is pretty as the first flower of spring."

'No, thank you. I have a place." Darla lifted her chin and stalked away, dragging the mule from the patch of grass he'd found by the porch. Despite her flippant response, tears stung the corners of her eyes. *Not even the saloons here would want me. I'd better not mess up at Downs House.* She tightened her fingers around the lead.

"I've brought you this far." A voice from deep inside of her being spoke.

Years before, Darla had heard Bible stories in Sunday school about people who heard the voice of God. But she'd never experienced it, and truly, had never thought of herself as the sort of person God would care to speak with. But somehow she knew it was Him. A warm feeling crept into her heart, like hot apple cider at Christmas or a hug from her father. She bowed her head. "Dear God," she said with a catch in her throat. "I'm sorry if I seemed ungrateful. I just don't want to ruin everything."

Footsteps thudded behind her. She whirled around to see Ethan.

His mouth was drawn down at the corners. "Darla, why did you wander all the way over here? I was worried when I came back and you were gone."

"Oh, I'm sorry. I was . . . reading these signs." Darla waved at the plaques decorating the front of the establishment.

Ethan studied the walls and his eyes widened. "I'm sure we could find you better things to read at the house." His eyes shifted from side to side and he lowered his voice. "It's probably best to stay away from this place. These ladies aren't very . . . nice."

Darla stumbled after the cart as they turned toward home. Her lips twitched, and a thought broke free from her mind and poured from her lips. "Stop me if I'm wrong," she heard herself say, "But didn't Christ spend time with sinners?"

Ethan turned and rubbed the back of his neck. "Well, now, yes, I'm sure I've heard a passage or two about that."

"And didn't He forgive a sinful woman? I'd bet she wasn't what most people would consider 'nice'.

A slow smile spread across Ethan's handsome face where a shadow of a beard was growing.

Darla fought a sudden urge to run a finger along his skin and feel those whiskers for herself. "Well now, shouldn't those folks be the ones Christians try to help? Aren't these the people you and your ma help every day? I didn't hear you asking for confessions before you ladled out soup in the street."

Ethan stopped short. "I can't argue with you there. But here's the problem: what if certain folks don't want help? If they chose to live that life, and they're fine and dandy with it?"

"That's true." Darla remembered the first time she'd met Soonie. She'd had no intention of leaving the saloon life, and probably never would have if Mr. Gandro hadn't beat the stuffing out of her.

Ethan turned and studied her. Pain glimmered in his eyes, along with hope, and kindness, and so many other things her mind found it hard to touch on.

Flutters of something she couldn't describe darted around in her chest. Perhaps because of the sincerity in his face. She hadn't been in the presence of a man she could trust since her daddy had passed away. Except for Brother Jenkins. *And he hardly counted.*

"Darla, I haven't known you very long, but I like learning more about you. You have such a kind spirit. The way you see people gives me a new perspective, even though I have been involved in charity work for most of my life. It's refreshing."

He touched her hand with one calloused finger, and her lips tingled with the notion that he might do it, he might bend down and kiss her right there on the street.

Instead he blinked and moved back, withdrawing his hand. "I'm sorry. I can't imagine what caused me to be so forward with you. You must not think I'm much of a gentleman."

"Oh no!" she blurted. "I would never think that."

"Please try not to run off any more, at least until you get your bearings in this city. Promise?"

"Sure." Part of Darla wanted to insist she could take care of herself in any place, at any time, without the help of any man. A piece of her heart felt satisfied and safe to walk beside this quiet, gentle man who cared for more than the parts of her he could steal away.

They continued down the street without further conversation, but Darla couldn't help humming a few bars from the whiskey hall's tune.

5

Church

The next several days passed faster than cards in the hands of a poker shark.

Darla didn't get a chance to work with Ethan again, though she went with the other women to hand out food. Occasionally he would join them at dinner table. When she asked Lisbeth about his whereabouts in the most innocent manner she could muster, the girl rolled her eyes and replied he was "making repairs."

After that, Darla noticed the banging sounds coming from the walls or under the floorboards at any given hour, or she would catch a glimpse of him striding through the fields, carrying boards or buckets of rocks.

It didn't take long for Darla to become accustomed to early mornings and days of chores. However, the first Sunday she nearly disgraced herself and all of Downs

House by nodding off in the second pew of Dallas Baptist Church.

As her chin touched the stiff collar of her dress, she started and blinked. Heat rose to her cheeks and she pretended to wipe a speck of dirt from the cover of her Bible.

"Holy, Holy, Holy!
though the darkness hide Thee,
Though the eye of sinful man,
Thy glory may not see:
Only Thou art holy,
there is none beside Thee,
Perfect in power, in love, and purity."

Despite her weariness, she savored the old hymn as the notes swelled from the organ. She closed her eyes and thought of her dad, tall and proud beside her in the family pew, singing the same song in his deep voice.

The minister shuffled to the front, leaning on a cane, his bald head shining in the light of lamps suspended from chains on the ceiling. When he reached the pulpit, he smiled out at the congregation and then began to quote a scripture.

"The Lord is my shepherd; I shall not want. He maketh me lie down in green pastures: he leadeth me beside the still waters . . ."

Darla found his tone comforting, and appreciated that the minister didn't shout and pound the pulpit like the pastor from the church when she was a child. *Though it might help me stay awake.*

During the sermon, she couldn't help sneaking glances at the people who shared her pew.

Indigo sat beside her, face unreadable as always. In all the hours they'd worked together, milking cows or mending clothes taken from the poor barrel, Darla hadn't been able to pry more than a few words from the woman. She wasn't sure if Indigo was addled in the head, or too shy to function.

Lisbeth sat between Indigo and Ma Downs, her long lashes fluttering against her cheeks while she mouthed a silent prayer.

Marnie and Sadie were staunch Presbyterians, so Ma Downs grudgingly allowed them to attend the church down the street. Mrs. Brodie suffered from a cold, so she had stayed home.

Ma Downs stood straight as a cornstalk, her head and ostrich plumes the only thing bent in any sort of submission. She sang and prayed with firm resolution, as though the entire church could be lost without her full participation.

Ethan anchored the group at the end of the pew. Occasionally, he would send a slanted look down the row, catch Darla's eye, and they would both turn their heads away.

Darla dared to glance his way again, just enough to see the collar of his shirt.

Instead of Ethan's amused eyes, she caught his mother's frown. Darla's face grew hot and she jerked her eyes to the front of the room where the patient minister was gesturing for the organist to play the final hymn.

As Darla sang, a thought crashed into the fine little castle she had built up for herself. *How can I think Ethan would care for me?* The idea was so crippling, her knees buckled a little. She steadied herself on the pew in front of her.

He doesn't know about my past. He doesn't know the occupation I've held, so disgraceful to society. She tried to swallow the lump in her throat. *I can't allow him to believe I'm a woman of upstanding morals. I might as well have 'Jezebel' written right across my forehead.*

The congregation bowed their collective heads for the closing prayer. The reverend's words poured out into the room, golden and smooth as new honey.

When the prayer ended, Darla followed the other bonnets as they bobbed out ahead of her.

The minister grasped Ma Downs by the hand when she went out the door in front of Darla.

"Mrs. Downs." His blue eyes twinkled under bushy white eyebrows. "How are you today? And what is this I've heard about you volunteering to head up the orphan's Christmas dinner again this year?"

"But of course." Ma Downs stiffened, her thin lips the only moving feature of her expressionless face. "I wouldn't miss the orphan's banquet."

The minister's smile sent waves through his wrinkled cheeks, and he adjusted his spectacles and glanced down the line behind Ma Downs at Darla and Lisbeth. "And I'm sure these ladies will help. Your house does such good work in this community, to assist the poor and show these unfortunate women how to be useful members of society. Is this a new one, then?" He took Darla's hand and shook it warmly. "Hello, my dear. I'm Reverend Martin."

Darla couldn't help but smile in return. "Yes, sir. I'm Darla North. Very pleased to meet you." She gave a little curtsy, and then reddened. *Is it proper to curtsy in church?*

"Let me welcome you to our city." Reverend Martin straightened his shirt front. "Are you finding it to your liking?"

"It ain't . . . isn't too shabby," said Darla. She glanced over at Ma Downs, whose eyes narrowed.

"Now, this old memory needs a bit of shaking. Did you mention where you came from?"

"No, Sir, I never did. A good day to you." Darla flashed him what she hoped was a dazzling smile and hurried out the door to join Lisbeth. The Irish girl was standing by a man in a black bowler hat, who prattled on and on about something.

Lisbeth's lips pressed into a smile so forced Darla was afraid they might be stuck that way forever.

Darla tugged at her sleeve. "Shall we go home?"

"Yes, please," Lisbeth sank against her.

"Another time?" Bowler Hat doffed his head covering, revealing a few sparse, greasy hairs.

Lisbeth gave him a withering look from behind her shawl and the two girls moved to the street.

On the way, they passed Ethan, who was talking to a middle-aged couple Darla had not yet been introduced to. A woman stood at his elbow and kept plucking at his arm. She threw back her head in response to something he said. Her perfect white teeth gleamed and brown curls cascaded down her back from under a fashionable Sunday bonnet.

"That man is insufferable," muttered Lisbeth, pulling Darla's attention from Ethan and his mysterious companions.

"Oh, you mean that fellow you were speaking to? Poor man. What's wrong with him?" asked Darla.

"Have you seen the way his lips turn down at the corners?" Lisbeth shook her head. "I can't watch him speak without thinking of a giant trout."

"Now that you mention it . . . that's exactly what he looks like! Oh dear." Darla put her hand up to her mouth. "Now I won't be able to speak to him either!"

The two women laughed so hard they were forced to stop and lean against each other in the street.

They sobered at the sight of Ma Downs barreling towards them, her face like a thundercloud.

"How could you be so rude?" she addressed Darla. Her voice broke as though she were on the verge of tears. "Reverend Martin was beside himself. He asked you a simple question, and could not understand why you were so short with him."

"Oh dear, I didn't mean it!" Darla wrung her hands. "I don't like talking about . . . where I came from. But I didn't mean to hurt his feelings."

Ma Downs's eyes softened, and to Darla's surprise, she reached out and smoothed the faded collar of the hideous cabbage-flower dress.

"You poor dear. Don't think you're the only one with a difficult past. All of the ladies, including myself, have been through the darkest moments imaginable."

Yes," Lisbeth said softly. "My daddy beat me, and years later, my husband did too. It's my good fortune they are both in their graves, or I'd be in mine, sure as sure."

Darla's shoulders sagged. *If only these kind women knew.* "I'm truly sorry," she said to Ma Downs. She squinted back down the road towards the church, already several blocks behind them. "I promise I'll apologize next Sunday."

"It's all right," said Ma Downs. Her pace quickened as they rounded the corner to the last street before home. "Now, ladies, we must discuss this Christmas banquet."

"Is the banquet at the orphanage?" Darla asked.

"Yes," said Ma Downs. "All the orphans come, along with the benefactors for Down's House."

"Benefactors?" Darla stepped around a particularly large puddle. "You mean the folks that give money?"

THE SALOON GIRL'S JOURNEY

"Yes. Did you see those people Ethan was speaking to out in the church yard?" Lisbeth pointed back down the lane. "The Bugle family has supported Down's House for fifteen years. They come to all our big events to make sure funds aren't spent in foolish or wasteful ways." She leaned toward Darla, lowering her voice. "Otherwise they might give the money to someone else."

Ma Downs stopped short in the road. "That is preposterous. They wouldn't do such a thing for any reason." She sighed. "However, it is important we do everything exactly right. No sense offending anyone." Sharp eyes settled on Darla. "Which means you need to be careful what you say, Missy."

Darla lowered her head. "Yes, Ma'am."

Lisbeth tugged on Darla's elbow and waited until Ma Downs was out of earshot. "If Ethan would go and marry the Bugle's daughter, Samantha, they'd never withdraw their support. That's what Ma Downs hopes. Then she wouldn't have to worry about keeping a roof over all of our heads."

"Samantha?" Darla remembered the beautiful girl hanging on to Ethan's arm. She shuddered.

Lisbeth laughed. "You should see your face. You look like the mama hog when someone bothers her babies."

Darla tried to look shocked. "Why would I worry myself about who Ethan's sweet on?"

Lisbeth raised her eyebrows but didn't reply.

Just the same, Samantha Bugle better watch out. Darla held on to this dark thought until she reached the gate of Downs House, where she repented and left it behind in the street.

6

Secrets

The sharp scent of cedar filled the parlor, where Darla, Lisbeth and Indigo fashioned wreaths from fresh boughs brought in from the nearby woods. The Pennel sisters and Mrs. Brodie were in the small room next to the parlor, which served for a sewing area, piecing together doll dresses. Each orphan girl would receive a handmade rag doll. Ethan had been whittling whistles and tops for the boys.

"Are we going to make shiny paper stars, or tie red ribbons on these?" Darla asked, holding up a prickly, fragrant wreath.

The other two women stared at her.

Indigo frowned. "No," she replied in her typical one-syllable response.

"Why not? Surely a few cents for paper could be spared." Darla held out the circlet and looked it over. "This seems so plain."

Lisbeth bit her lip and focused on her work.

Patience, who had been allowed a rare break from housework to help with preparations for the festivities, popped up from her place on the floor where she was clipping branches into the proper length. "Miss Darla, we don't ever have money to spare."

"No, not in the two Christmases I've been here. It's always been a pretty plain affair." Lisbeth said. The pile of branches by her foot shifted and Danny poked up his furry face, cheeks round with the acorns he'd been stuffing into it.

"Hide Danny." Indigo pointed to the animal.

"Ma won't be back from the market for ages." Lisbeth waved her hand. "He's fine for now."

Indigo shook her head, wrinkles furrowing above her eyebrows. All the ladies in the house played with Danny and helped to hide him from Ma Downs, but Darla knew they also thought Lisbeth took too many chances. Privately, she agreed, but she'd already learned when Lisbeth had a mind to do something, not much would change it.

Darla tried again. "These orphans, they have such little joy and color in their lives. Even at the sa—at the place I used to live, we decorated every free surface with any ornaments we could get our hands on."

Patience's head bobbed up again. "I have lots of paper, Miss Darla. It might work all right."

"Really?" Darla clasped her hands. "Would you show me?"

Patience darted a look at Lisbeth, and her beautiful brown eyes widened. "The papers are in my room. A fancy lady like you might not want to come in there."

"Fancy?" Darla rolled her eyes. "Silly girl. I'm not a bit fancy. I didn't pick out this face or these blond curls for myself. God did. Could you please show me your papers, Patience?"

The little girl sighed and went to the door. "Come this way, Miss Darla."

Brushing pine needles from her dress, Darla nodded to Lisbeth and Indigo. "I'll be right back."

Lisbeth made a noise in the back of her throat but said nothing.

She's not the only one who's stubborn. Darla lifted her chin and swept out of the room.

The house was divided by a long narrow open-air section Ma Downs called a 'dog-trot,' though Darla doubted a dog had ever set foot in the home. One side held the bedrooms, parlor and entry way, the other half had the kitchen, dining area, washroom, and storage.

Patience beckoned to her. "This way, Miss Darla. Let's hurry." The little girl craned her neck to look over her shoulder. "I want to be back in here before Mrs. Downs comes home."

"Why are you so worried?" Darla picked up her skirts to keep up. "It's a project for the orphans' banquet, and she asked us to help."

The girl didn't answer, just pushed open the door to the kitchen.

Darla had only been in the kitchen a few times. This part of the house was the territory of Mrs. Betty, Patience's mother, and she didn't take kindly to unfortunates disturbing her kingdom of flaky pies, steaming soup, and stacks of clean dishes. Rows of gleaming pots hung from a metal contraption suspended from the ceiling. Wooden cabinets with peeling white paint lined the walls.

Mrs. Betty, a short, plump woman with umber skin and a stiff, starched apron, stirred something in a pot on the stove and hummed to herself.

As Darla and Patience clattered around the counter, she turned and put a hand on her hip. "Patience, what are you doing bringing Miss Fancy back here?"

"Your daughter wanted to show me something in her room, if that's all right. And I'm really not fancy, I'm just a person," said Darla, not sure if she should feel offended or amused. She resisted the impulse to stick her finger in a nearby bowl of what appeared to be cookie batter.

Mrs. Betty squinted at her. "You're fancy 'cause I said so." She pulled a tray of biscuits from the stove and slammed shut the cast iron door. "You'd better not let Mrs. Downs catch you in here. I don't need no unfortunates gallivanting through my casseroles and swiping pies."

Darla gave the cookie dough one last, lingering look. "I promise I won't touch anything."

Patience patted Mrs. Betty's large, capable arm. "Mama, please don't tell Mrs. Downs. It's a surprise. For the orphans."

"Hmmph." Mrs. Betty dumped the biscuits on a plate.

The smell wafted into Darla's senses and made her mouth water.

"You won't catch me being a tattle-tale," Mrs. Betty continued. "But it's gonna get you into hot water if you try to change any part of that hoity-toity banquet. Believe you me."

Goodness, all we want to do is cut out a few paper stars. Darla shook her head and followed Patience through a small door and into a narrow room full of shelves and boxes. The little girl stopped to select a lantern from a row on the shelf. After lighting the wick, she went into yet another room. At first, Darla thought they were in a cupboard, but it had no shelves this time. *It must be a hallway.* She tried to retrace their steps and figure out where they were in the house, but she would have been hopelessly lost if it weren't for Patience.

The girl paused at a set of narrow doors. "Right through here," she said, a hint of pride in her voice. "Mrs. Downs said I could share a room with my Mama, but when I found out this larder wasn't being used anymore, I asked if I could have it for my own and Mrs. Downs said yes." Ducking her head down, she smiled. "I'd never had anything all my own before."

She pulled open the door.

It was a squeeze pushing Darla's skirts and petticoats through the entry way, but at last she made it inside.

Patience set down her lantern on a small table. Everywhere the light touched, colors blazed. The small cot was covered in a crazy quilt, pieced together from fabrics of every color and texture. And the walls . . . Darla lifted the lantern high for a closer look. The walls were covered with bits of paper, scraps of tin beaten into diamonds and hearts, newspaper and catalogue pages. Some were painted over with bright designs of butterflies and flowers and ladies dancing.

"Patience, this is beautiful. Did you do all of this yourself?"

Patience nodded. "All except for the quilt. Lisbeth helped me make it." She pulled a small wooden box from beneath the cot and began to rummage through it. "These are nice." The little girl held up bright sheets of tissue. "We could twist these into flowers, maybe."

"Flowers? That would be lovely."

"And perhaps we could cut out paper chains from this. They're only printed words, but they might be nice." Patience fanned through sheets of newspaper.

"It's hard to believe you're only twelve. You have so many wonderful ideas," said Darla. "And your paintings are good as most I've seen by grown folks."

"You think so?" Patience cupped her chin in her hands. "I don't have much time for them, but my head aches if I can't paint sometimes."

"It must be what you were born to do," Darla declared, piling the papers back into the box. "My daddy always said God has a purpose for each one of us."

Patience frowned. "That would be nice, Miss Darla, but most folks aren't going to give two pennies for a colored girl's paintings."

Darla sighed. She wished she could argue, but in her heart she knew it was true. "Well, it's just horrible," she finally said. "People wouldn't know good sense if it slapped them in the face."

"Anyway," Patience said brightly, "at least we can make a nice Christmas for the orphans."

"I have some white tissue upstairs. We'll cut snowflakes from that," Darla continued. "The girls at the sa-- the place I used to live showed me how."

"It will look like Heaven and fairyland all rolled into one," said Patience, with a wistful smile.

"Oh, no." Darla reached for her hand. "You won't get to come, will you?"

"No." Patience stared down at the table. "Mama always says I'm too young."

"Well, perhaps this year will be different." Darla traced the petals of a bright flower painted over a soap advertisement. "I could use your help to make sure everything turns out perfectly."

Patience beamed. "That would be nice."

Darla's stomach growled loudly. "You think your mama might spare one of those biscuits?" she whispered.

"She just might," Patience whispered back.

The little girl picked up the lantern, and Darla followed her back through the tiny, dark hallway and into the warm kitchen.

Warm, golden biscuits were stacked in a bowl. Darla reached for one, but Mrs. Betty's wooden spoon smacked down on her hand before she could close her fingers around the treat.

"Ow!" Darla put her finger in her mouth.

"Ow is right." Mrs. Betty shook her spoon. "You'll get some at supper time, same as everyone else. Now you two skeedaddle out of my kitchen."

The door creaked open behind them. The light scent of sawdust and pine filled Darla's senses as Ethan leaned over the counter in front of her. He'd come in from the kitchen porch and hadn't bothered to take off the long, leather duster he'd started wearing ever since the weather cooled.

"Don't mind me, ladies, just came in to wash up in here where it's warm." He pumped the handle up and down a few times until a thin stream of water ran into the sink.

"Aw, we never mind you, Mr. Ethan." Mrs. Betty reached over to pinch Ethan's cheek, a gesture so absurd on the chiseled face that Darla had to stifle a giggle. "He's been coming in this kitchen since before he wore breeches, haven't you?"

"Sure, I have." Ethan dried his hands on a flour sack hanging on a nail and reached for a biscuit. "Mind if I take one of these, Mrs. Betty?"

Darla's eyes followed the spoon as it settled peacefully back into the bowl of batter.

Mrs. Betty smiled. "Of course not, dear. You need your strength. You work so hard out there."

Ethan grabbed a roll and twitched it behind his back where Mrs. Betty couldn't see.

Darla snatched the biscuit and hid it in her apron pocket. The bread warmed her skin through the material.

Giving the girls a wink, Ethan nodded to Mrs. Betty. "All right, ladies, we better get out of the kitchen so this talented woman here can finish up with the food."

Darla flashed him her brightest smile. "I'll see you at supper. I'd better go check on my decorating committee."

She left the kitchen and stopped in the dog trot to eat her purloined biscuit. The crumbs melted as soon as they touched her tongue. Mrs. Betty could make even the simplest fare taste like magic.

"Oh, there you are!" Lisbeth called from the door.

Darla brushed a few crumbs from her face, along with, she hoped, her guilty expression. She turned to see not only Lisbeth, but Ma Downs enter the dogtrot.

"Hello," said Darla. "I was just coming in to check on the wreaths."

"Yes, we're almost finished." Lisbeth turned back towards the parlor entrance.

A furry head poked out from beneath Lisbeth's shawl.

Danny? Darla drew a sharp breath and darted a glance at Ma Downs, who stopped to examine the wall.

"Lisbeth, come here at once." Ma Downs' voice had a steel edge to it.

Lisbeth moved past Darla, who fought the urge to grab Danny and run off in the opposite direction to prevent his discovery. However, she wasn't quite sure what the creature would do to her if she laid sudden hands on him, so she chose instead to send up a quick prayer that perhaps the animal had not been detected.

She ducked her head and passed the ladies to enter the parlor door.

"Lisbeth, tell me, does this paneling look rotted to you?" The words floated after Darla, and she breathed a sigh of relief.

"I don't think so," came Lisbeth's response. "But perhaps Ethan should look at it."

"Fine. Now would you please go take that animal back to your room? I don't want him loose in the halls."

Darla's eyes widened, and she shook her head. *Can't get anything past that woman. She probably knew about Danny from the day Lisbeth found him.*

7

Christmas

*M*usty air wafted out from the Chadwick Orphanage dining hall as Darla, Indigo, Lisbeth and the Pennel sisters arrived, their arms full of boxes and bundles.

Four long tables, lined with rough, serviceable chairs, sat in rows through the large room. A dirty window at the end of the room was the only source of light.

How can they even see to eat? If it was anything like the orphanage Darla had grown up in, the children wouldn't have much light from candles or lanterns either. Of course, light had only made it easier to see weevils crawling in the bread. *God, thank you I don't have to live in a place like this anymore.* She glanced at the sisters. Their eyes were wide, and for once they weren't giggling. *That's right. They also grew up in an orphanage.*

"What a dismal place," Lisbeth murmured as she unpacked a bundle of wreaths.

"Yes, but we'll brighten it up." Darla said in the most cheerful tone she could muster. "When I lived in an orphanage, we never had a special meal for Christmas or any time."

In the orphanage, the only indication of Christmas was the carols they sang at church. The nuns who ran the orphanage would hurry them through the streets, not allowing the children to even stop and look in the store windows. Sudden tears pricked Darla's eyes.

Work at Downs House wasn't easy, but she loved the chance to serve people in need. Not lonely cowboys who probably had faithful wives waiting for them at home, but people who were starved for love and care.

She put the packages down on the nearest table. "Are any of the workers here going to help us?" she asked Indigo.

"No." Indigo's eyes traveled over the walls and floor. "Dirty."

"They're too busy herding children." Lisbeth twisted a strand of hair around her finger. "I wish we had time to scrub the place down, but at least we can take a few minutes to clean the worst of it. No sense planting roses in a pigsty."

The women cleaned the window, dusted the tables and swept out the room with a bedraggled broom Marnic found in the corner.

"Girls, we'll have to hurry if we want to get all these pretties up before the children arrive." Darla pulled out a handful of tissue snowflakes, almost as fragile as the real things.

Lisbeth stared at the snowflakes. "I still don't know if we should put up all the decorations, Darla. You've only been here a short time. You haven't seen what it's like when the benefactors come on an inspection."

Darla sighed. "If we get in trouble, I'll take the blame. All right?" She surveyed the other women's faces.

"It would have been nice if someone had made a special Christmas for us, just once." Sadie picked up a snowflake. "Darla, where would you like to hang these?"

"Hmmm . . ." Darla turned, studying the room. "Perhaps we could string them up over here." She ran to the side wall, where paintings of past benefactors glared down at them.

"I'll get started." Sadie grabbed a chair from a table and climbed up to string the decorations.

"Marnie and Lisbeth, should we have four candles per table, or two?" asked Darla.

Marnie drummed her finger against a plump cheek. "I don't know. What do you think, Lisbeth?"

Lisbeth tossed her hair. "All I know is Ma Downs will have a living fit when she finds out you're wasting perfectly good candles."

"Oh, don't be silly," Darla protested. "Patience found them at the back of the tool shed. They'd been there for years. Ethan said it was a wonder that mice hadn't gotten them. I think it was truly fortunate." She took a deep breath. *Would the benefactors really make a fuss over a few candles?*

Ethan pushed through the door carrying a lovely little evergreen tree they'd found in the woods behind the cow pasture. "Where would you like this to go, ma'am?" he asked Darla. "Whew! These needles are sharp!"

"Right there in the corner, please, sir." Darla waved to the spot. "And do you think you could set it up for us?"

"Anything for you."

A knowing look passed between Marnie and Sadie, and they went into a fit of giggles.

Darla's cheeks grew warm, but she squared her shoulders and continued to hang snowflakes. *So he has a little crush on me. It's nothing but a bit of harmless fun. Not that I mind getting attention from a man with good morals for once.*

A cry of dismay from Indigo interrupted her thoughts. She looked up to see her struggling with a tangled popcorn string.

"I'm coming." Darla rushed over and picked at the string until it came free, with only a few snowy kernels lost.

An hour later, Darla surveyed the room with satisfaction. Colorful paper chains draped over the tree's branches, along with strings of popcorn. Evergreen wreaths lined the room, chasing away the scent of mold and must. Tin-can stars, polished until they shone like costly silver, dripped from the wreaths. Candles blazed on the tables, and a gleaming round orange had been placed beside each plate.

Lisbeth and Indigo stood silent with shining eyes.

Sadie clasped her hands and said, "Isn't it wonderful? It's all so wonderful!"

Ethan surveyed the room. "It's the best it's ever been." He caught Darla's eye. "You did a great job.'

Darla's smile hurt her cheeks. "We all worked together. It wasn't just me."

"But you had the best ideas," said Lisbeth.

A knock came at the door, and Ethan went to open it.

A middle-aged couple Darla was sure she recognized entered the room. Following them was a woman wearing a very stiff black crepe dress with puffed sleeves that almost brushed her ears and a starched collar. Ma Downs came in behind her. Last in was a young woman with snapping eyes and brown curls that settled like sausages on her shoulders.

Oh yes, how could I forget? Darla's shoulders sagged. *Samantha Bugle.* The Bugles were benefactors. Of course they would attend the supper.

"May I take your coats?" Lisbeth stepped forward.

Samantha shrugged off her mink coat to reveal a stunning cranberry velvet gown. She handed her coat to Lisbeth without a word of thanks.

Darla looked down at her own shapeless dress, suddenly conscious of how very dirty and disheveled she must look after the afternoon's work.

"Hello, ladies, we have come to see your progress," said Ma Downs. "Most of you have met Mr. and Mrs. Bugle, and this is Miss Comfort, the orphanage director."

"And I'm Samantha Bugle," the young woman said, her eyes fixed on Darla.

Darla supposed she was addressing her, but the girl swept up to Ethan and held out a gloved hand. "How are you this evening, Mr. Downs?"

Ethan stared at the offered hand and finally shook it with limp fingers. "I'm fine, Miss Bugle."

"Oh!" came from Ma Downs. She stood as if rooted to the floor, staring at the Christmas finery around her.

Darla tore her eyes away from Samantha, who she had privately labeled 'the snoot' and went to stand by Ma Downs. "We just now finished with the decorations. Do you like it?"

Ma Downs continued to stare, her eyes widening. "Why, Darla, it's just . . . just . . ."

"Preposterous," Mr. Bugle broke in, waving a black cane topped with a brass knob. "How much money was wasted on all this frippery? Those coppers should have been spent on food, or clothes."

"Absolutely right, Daddy." Samantha adjusted her gloves. "After all, orphans shouldn't have things too nice. They might start expecting more handouts."

"If this is the way the hard-earned money of Downs House benefactors is being spent, perhaps it should be better placed," Mr. Bugle said to his wife, a plump woman with clouds of white hair who had yet to speak.

Darla caught a knowing glance from Lisbeth and sucked in a breath. Should she even try to argue? They hadn't spent a cent of money on decorations, just time and hard work. *And the Bugles haven't even seen the gifts by the tree.*

Ethan moved to her side. "If I may have a word, Mr. Bugle." He spoke in an even tone, but his fists were clenched by his sides.

Ma Downs stretched out a trembling hand towards her son. "Yes, Ethan, could you please explain?"

Darla had never seen her with such lost composure, even the other day with Reverend Martin.

"Mr. Bugle." Ethan swept his arm out. "Every decoration here was hand-made by these ladies, including the gifts under the tree. The supplies came from odds and ends destined for the trash barrel, and even from the woods. The only thing purchased was a ball of twine to hang things, and I used my own funds for that."

"Even so," Mr. Bugle blustered, "these are orphans. They must learn that life isn't all about gumdrops and rainbows."

"Oh, Daddy." Samantha purred, "If Ethan's in charge, it must be all right." She gave Ethan a simpering smile that made Darla's stomach clench.

Miss Comfort, whom Darla had almost forgotten, moved out from behind Mrs. Bugle and took Darla's hand. "It looks lovely," she said in a voice barely above a whisper.

"The children will be so delighted. How can I ever thank you?" A tear gleamed in the corner of her eye.

"I was an orphan myself, and all of us ladies have been through hard times," said Darla. "It was our pleasure." She gave a defiant glance at Samantha, who pursed her lips and looked as though she was tempted to stick out her tongue.

Ma Downs stood a little straighter and went to the door. "Well, Ms. Comfort, there are two dozen hungry children waiting outside. Should we call them in for supper?"

The boys entered first, shoulders squared, standing tall like soldiers. The little girls followed them, walking in dignified grace. Despite their effort, tiny squeals escaped from their lips as they saw the beautiful decorations.

I don't care. I don't care if I get thrown out on the street for this. Darla decided. *It was worth it.* And suddenly she felt a stirring in her heart that had never been there before. *I have a purpose. I am useful in this world, and God has a calling for me. Despite my past. He has truly forgiven me.*

She was tempted to kneel down right there on the floor and thank God for His goodness and mercy, but she didn't think it would go over well with the Bugles.

Behind the parade of orphans came Mrs. Betty, carrying a large covered skillet, and with her, Patience.

"You came!" Darla ran to her and took one of the baskets hanging from the little girl's arm.

"Yes." Patience's big brown eyes shone in the candlelight. 'Mama said I was old enough this year." She sat her load on the table. "And look at these." Pulling out a small parcel from a basket, she revealed four cloth butterflies, painted with brilliant colors. "Cut them from a flour sack this afternoon."

Darla clasped her hands. "How lovely! Let's hang them from the tree."

After the little girls and boys ate every crumb of the simple but delicious supper, everyone gathered around the Christmas tree. The presents were passed out, and sounds of tearing paper and shrieks of joy filled the banquet hall. The dolls were tiny masterpieces, each with two hand-sewn dresses created by Lisbeth. The boys' wooden whistles had been painted by Patience.

After the presents were opened, Mr. Bugle gave in to the spirit of the day long enough to read the story of Christ's birth from the Bible and even led a warbling version of 'Oh Come, All Ye Faithful."

Where did Ethan go? He'd been by Darla's side a moment ago. She scanned the faces. Her eyes rested on Samantha's scowl. *At least* she's *not with him. Darla North, you're acting like a school girl.*

The door opened, and Ethan came in with a battered fiddle. He held it up and everyone clapped and cheered.

Darla stared at him. She'd had no idea he could play. *Stands to reason. He makes lovely carvings with wood, why not have the ability to create music as well?*

The first slide of the bow across the strings brought notes sweet and clear, which strung together into an old carol. Songs tumbled from the instrument, one after the other.

During the music, Darla found herself longing to climb into the fiddle and float away on the melody, to become part of the song. She inched closer and closer to Ethan, until she was right beside him. *If only I could rest my head on his shoulder.*

Her eyes met Samantha Bugle's chilly stare, and she stopped short. She was almost tempted to check her heart and make sure it was still beating. Recovering, she returned the glare with a cool gaze. *I'm pretty sure he likes me better than you, and there's nothing you can do about it.*

As the last note from the fiddle died away, the children's eyes began to droop and a few of them rested against the walls or shoulders.

Ethan smiled down on them. "Just one more, and then you may all go to bed." He lifted the instrument again. Everyone, even Samantha, joined in to sing the beautiful song.

What child is this?
Who laid to rest,
on Mary's lap is sleeping?

Darla's lips trembled as she sang, and the melody sent shivers up her spine. She caught Ethan's eye, and he winked at her over his fiddle.

On the walk home from the orphanage under the twinkling stars, Ethan came to walk beside her. He pressed something into her hand. The moonlight revealed the little wooden rose, polished and perfect.

"Oh, thank you," she whispered. "You didn't have to."

"I didn't forget." His smile shone from beneath the brim of his hat.

Darla's fingers trembled; she wanted to hold his hand so badly. Instead she clenched her fists and shoved them into the pockets of her pinafore.

It had been the best Christmas of her entire life.

8

Illness

Snow came in late January, normal for north Texas. Darla paused on her way to feed the pigs to watch an early calf frolic in the cold flurry. Sun sparkled on the white blanket that covered the house, grounds and outbuildings.

"Now I want to lie down and make a snow angel," she said to Lisbeth, and Indigo, who passed by carrying pails and bundles.

"Too cold," said Indigo with a frown.

"Yep. Don't get any notions in your head," Lisbeth said. "You'll catch a chill, like Ethan."

"Ethan's sick?" Darla hadn't heard the news. True, she hadn't seen Ethan around the house, but she'd just assumed he was busy elsewhere.

"Yes. Nothing serious. Ma Downs doesn't want to call for a doctor just yet, but she made him go home and rest."

Lisbeth held up her pail. "We're taking him some soup. Ma Downs always has us ladies go to his house in pairs . . . proprieties' sake and all."

I've never seen his house. Darla knew Ethan lived in a little cabin out in the back acreage, but she'd never had an excuse to go there. She was seized by a sudden desire to peek inside and learn more about this quiet, kind man who'd taken her fancy. *Plus, I want to see how sick he is for myself. I hope it truly is nothing serious.*

"Indigo, would you mind taking this to the pigs for me?" she coaxed. "I want to check on Ethan. Please?"

Indigo's face clouded, her scar darkening like it always did when she was upset. "Why?"

"Well . . . because I want to see his house. I never have. Please, Indigo?"

Indigo shook her head. "Dirty."

"Oh, come on Indigo. If you let me go, I'll . . ."

"How about she feeds the pigs for a week when it's your turn?" Lisbeth said.

"Fine." Indigo snatched the slop bucket away from Darla and shoved her bundle into Darla's hands. She turned and shuffled off in the direction of the pigpen.

"Goodness, I didn't realize she hated pigs so much." A few drops of slop had landed on Darla's hand in the exchange, and she rubbed her skin with snow to clean it.

"It's not just the pigs . . . she doesn't like changes." Lisbeth started down a little path that led behind the barn to a thick stand of trees in the back of the property. "Even the tiniest difference can upset her. It's just the way she is."

"Oh. Well, I didn't mean to make her mad." Darla paused for a moment to stare at the tree branches dripping with icicles. The forest had been transformed into a fairy palace. She hoped Ethan would be well enough to come see it. "I've always wondered . . . how did she get that scar, anyway?"

Lisbeth froze. "I've never asked. You know she doesn't talk much anyway. Ma Downs told me she found her in the poorhouse. It must have been right after it happened. She was curled up in the corner with a dirty rag wrapped 'round her face. Wouldn't let a doctor touch her, even though the folks at the poorhouse tried. Somehow, Ma Downs got her home and convinced her that she could be trusted. The wound turned septic and Indigo almost died. I can't imagine how painful it must have been. But she pulled through."

Darla shuddered and touched her own face. "How terrible." Suddenly the bumps and bruises Darla had received over the years seemed paltry. She resolved in her heart to be more patient with Indigo, whose strange habits could be frustrating sometimes.

The cabin was nestled in a small grove of evergreen trees. Their bright needles peeped through the snow. Smoke puffed from the chimney, and a fresh set of tracks ran from the door to the woodpile and back again.

"He's not dead, anyway," Lisbeth muttered. She gave Darla her pixie smile.

"I should hope not!" Darla knocked on the thick door which had been fashioned from split logs and hung with giant hinges that looked as though they'd come from the door of a railroad car.

"Come in." Ethan's voice drifted through the wall.

He doesn't sound very good. Darla took a deep breath and pushed the door open.

A cloud of warmth beckoned them in to the tiny room. A cozy fire crackled merrily in the stone fireplace, and the flame from a lantern's tiny wick danced and flickered in its globe. Ethan's old fiddle gleamed from a place of honor on an ornately carved mantel that seemed far too grand for the room. Wood carvings had been placed all over the room, animals and flowers and trees, each one more beautiful than the last.

"Hello," Ethan said in a shaky voice. He was propped up in a bed in the corner, his normally tanned cheeks pale and hollow. His curls were plastered to his forehead, and he brushed his hand through them and straightened his shoulders. "Hey, Darla, I didn't know you were coming to see me."

"Of course I came." Darla rushed to his side and reached behind to fluff the flattened pillow behind him. The thick cotton was drenched in sweat. "Oh, looks like you've been running a fever."

"We brought you some soup." Lisbeth placed the pail on a stool nearby and pried the loaf of bread away from Darla, who still had it tucked tightly beneath her arm. "And I saw those tracks. Ethan Downs, you had no business going out in the snow!"

"Eh." Ethan waved off the words with a trembling hand. "I'm doing much better now. Should've seen me yesterday. Couldn't even get out of bed. The fire was going down. I couldn't let it go out, could I?"

"You knew very well we were coming over to check on you. Wait next time," Lisbeth scolded.

Without thinking, Darla laid the back of her hand against Ethan's forehead. "You do feel hot. She's right. You shouldn't be outside."

Ethan closed his eyes. "Your hand is cool. It feels nice."

Darla's face grew hot and she drew her hand back. She looked over at Lisbeth. "I'm sorry. I just wanted to see . . ."

Lisbeth raised her eyebrows. "He does look better than yesterday. Still, we'll have to set up a watch if he's going to be trying to traipse off out in the cold. I need to tell Ma Downs. Can I leave you here for a few moments?"

"I'll take care of him," Darla promised.

"Uh huh. I'm sure you will." Lisbeth slammed the door behind her.

Ethan lowered back on the bed. "Thanks for staying with me. I know everyone has work to do, and more of it since I haven't been able to pull my weight. But it's been lonely out here."

"How long have you been sick?"

"I don't know. What's today? Ma sent me to bed on Sunday."

"You've been sick for three days? Oh, Ethan, I'm sorry. No one told me, or I would have figured out a way to check on you sooner."

His dry lips cracked into a smile. "I just bet you would have."

A jug of water stood nearby, and Darla poured some into a cup and held it for him.

He managed a few swallows. "Thank you."

"Of course."

"You're an angel, you know that? A golden-haired, blue-eyed angel." His eyes were half-closed, his voice soft.

Darla bit back a snort of laughter. *An angel from a saloon? Not likely.* "You're sweet to say so."

"I know so." Ethan leaned back and closed his eyes.

Poor man. Oh, I hope he gets better soon. Darla's mind raced. She'd seen her share of sick folks. One saloon girl had passed away from a fever while Darla was holding her hand. *Surely Ma Downs will know if something more should be done.*

She stood and walked over to a shelf on the wall. Leaning forward, she studied some of the carvings there, almost afraid to breathe lest she knock over a delicate figure and cause irreparable damage.

An elephant and a tiger shared space with a pig and a giraffe. They were all made from the same dark, coarse wood, and these figures were more crudely fashioned than the other work she had seen from Ethan.

"Those are some of my earliest carvings," Ethan said from the bed. "My brother gave me my first pocket knife when I was eight, and I carved up everything I could get my hands on. Got me into all kinds of trouble." He gave a weak chuckle, which ended in a coughing fit.

Darla hurried back over. "Please don't try to talk too much, you really should rest."

"Can you do something for me?"

"Of course, Ethan."

"Will you sing?"

"You might not like my voice."

Ethan rolled over to face the wall so all she saw was his curly hair peeping from beneath the quilt. "I bet I will. I hear you in church, you know."

Darla began on the first song that rose to her mind, an old hymn her father used to sing.

"Fair are the meadows, fairer still the woodlands,
Robed in the blooming garb of spring;
Jesus is fairer, Jesus is purer,
Who makes the woeful heart to sing."

"Wish I could play my fiddle," Ethan murmured.

"Me too," said Darla.

She went on with the next part.

"Fair is the sunshine,
Fairer still the moonlight,

And all the twinkling starry host;
Jesus shines brighter, Jesus shines purer
Than all the angels heaven can boast."

The door burst open, and Ma Downs bustled in, carrying an armload of blankets. Mrs. Betty followed, lugging a small skillet with round stones inside.

Ethan turned over and blinked. "Hey, Ma."

"Miss North, I thank you for staying with my son since he seems intent on catching his death," Ma Downs glared at Ethan. "But it's hardly proper for you to be here alone."

"I—I'm sorry. We didn't know what else to do," said Darla.

"You could have come in with Lisbeth," said Ma Downs. "What if the benefactors find out? They'll accuse us of running a house of ill-repute."

Darla's heart pounded in her chest. "I was just watching him so he wouldn't go outside again. Didn't Lisbeth tell you?"

"Can't the sick fetch a little firewood?" Ethan protested. "I'm much better today, Ma."

Ma Downs put her hands on her hips. "You do look better," she admitted. "But if I catch you outside again . . . I'll . . ."

"I'd give him a hiding like I used to, if he weren't a grown man now," said Mrs. Betty.

Ma Downs turned to Darla. "Go on home now. We'll let you know if we need anything else. And I don't want you or any of the other girls out here again. Mrs. Betty and I will bring out anything he needs from now on."

Darla sighed. "Get better," she whispered to Ethan.

"Of course I will."

9

A Day at the Fair

"You'll go with me, won't you?"

Darla jumped. "Jehosaphat! Ethan, you gave me a fright!" She fluttered earth-covered fingers before her face.

"Sorry." He knelt down beside her to examine the neatly sown rows of carrots she'd been planting. "How long have you been out here?"

"Since after breakfast. I should be finished with these carrots by lunch time, especially if I have some help." Ever since Ethan's illness, Darla had stopped trying to ignore the sweetness smoldering between them, though neither one had acknowledged their feelings in words. *And I'm fine with this. I'm happy with the way things are,* she reminded herself.

The last thing Darla wanted was to lose the trust she had worked so hard to build with Ma Downs. And Darla hadn't missed the woman's raised eyebrows and pursed lips every time she caught the two of them flirting.

Ethan wiped off his hands. "Sorry, I can't stay long. I just came by to ask if you'd decided to come with me today." His chin was covered in stubble, and again she fought the urge to run her finger along his face while he talked. *But I'm not that kind of woman anymore. I'm fine. Fine.* She clenched the packet of seeds so tightly it burst, and a shower of carrot seeds flew into the air.

"Oh goodness, look what I've done!" She tried to scoop the tiny seeds back into the packet.

Ethan laughed and helped her scoop up the mess. "We'll just have a big batch of carrots in one place. People will come for miles to see the giant mystery clump. They'll wonder why some farmer decided to plant so many in one spot."

"Oh stop . . ." Darla went into a gale of laughter, leaning against the fence. She wiped her eyes and looked up. Ethan was staring at her, eyes softened, his lips curled into a smile.

He cares for me more than I thought. The realization hit her like a wagon load of rocks. She turned away, pretending to focus on covering the scattered seeds with dirt. *But he couldn't love me if he knew.* She wiped dirt from her fingers. *It's wicked of me to deceive him . . . but I can't let him find out the truth, he might tell Ma Downs and then I'd be out of here in two shakes of a rattler's tail. No matter what she said before, I know she wouldn't want a saloon girl in her house. Or flirting with her son.* Where would she go? She'd learned so much here, and helped so many people.

"Hello." A tan hand waved in front of her eyes. "Is Princess Darla off in Dreamland?" Ethan tipped his head to the side.

"Oh." Darla blinked. "I'm sorry. You were asking me a question, weren't you? You wanted me to go somewhere with you?" Her shoulders sagged. "Did the cow get bogged down in the pond again?"

"No, silly. Don't you remember? I told you about the little fair in town, a mile away. It's a bit soggy still. I'll never understand why they plan these things in March--but I bet we'll have fun anyway." Ethan rested his chin on folded hands. "Please say you'll go with me."

Darla bit her lip. "But what about your ma? Will she let me have the day off?"

He raised an eyebrow. "Darla, you've been working yourself to death ever since you arrived here. We all work hard. Everyone deserves a break every once in awhile, don't you think?"

She opened her mouth, and the protest must have reached her eyes because he held up a hand.

"Don't worry about Ma. I'll see if I can convince her to give half the girls a few hours off today, and the other three can go tomorrow. She knows young ladies need some fun. After all, she was young once," he said with a hint of doubt in his tone. He leaned closer, and Darla breathed in the sawdust-honey scent that was all his own. "Come on, Darla."

We're here and now. Who knows where I'll be in the next month? Or even a week. "Of course I'll come. How could I say no to the most handsome man in town?"

His eyes widened, and a grin spread over his face. "All right, we'll leave after lunch. Maybe the sun will have time to dry the worst puddles."

After he left, Darla finished with the carrots and went to the pump at the side of the house to wash her hands.

Ethan's voice floated over the porch railing. "Ma, some of the ladies have been asking for a half day, and I thought today might be good for it."

Darla heard a sigh. "Don't we need to get the back pasture cleared?"

"The pasture isn't going anywhere. Everyone's been working so hard with planting. They need a break. Let them go."

"I suppose you're right, son. I'll let Indigo, Mrs. Brodie and Darla go today, and everyone else can go tomorrow. I simply cannot spare them all at once."

Darla ducked in the side door before anyone could find her eavesdropping. She was disappointed Lisbeth couldn't come with them to the fair. *I'll bring a few pennies and buy her a trinket.*

Attempts to contain her excitement through lunch proved successful, all except for one foot that would tap the floor in a brisk rhythm no matter how many times she stilled it. Lisbeth raised her eyebrows at her a few times, but no one else seemed to notice.

After the meal, Darla hastened upstairs and looked over her few possessions.

She'd used some of the money from Soonie's five-dollar gold piece to buy items of clothing that fit, decent under things, and hair ribbons for church. Her favorite purchase was a smart little hat, with black feathers and an artificial flower on the top. She pushed a hat pin through the velvet surface to make sure the hat wouldn't be lost in an errant wind and pinched her cheeks. Narrowing her eyes in the mirror, she sighed. *This will have to do. Any more fancy primping and someone will get suspicious.*

Ma Downs had been gracious to give the half day, but Darla doubted she had any notion that she and Ethan were going off together. *Though he should be free to do what he wants. He's a grown man.*

As she reached for the door handle, someone turned it from the other side. Lisbeth pushed her way into the room.

Danny scampered out from under the bed and settled on his owner's shoulder, chattering.

"Did you decide where you're going for your half-day?" Lisbeth asked as she fed the squirrel bits of bread from lunch.

"Ethan asked me to go to the fair," Darla said. *Lisbeth isn't a snitch. And we aren't doing anything wrong.*

"I see. Well, have a good time." Lisbeth's lips curved up into her usual pixie smile.

"Please don't tell Ma Downs we're going together." Darla begged.

Lisbeth tossed her red braid over her shoulder, almost knocking Danny from his perch. "The biggest simpleton in the world could see what's going on. I don't know why you're trying to be all hush-hush about it anyway."

"I have my reasons." Darla tipped up her chin and went out the door.

"She's a minx, but she's our friend, isn't she, Danny?" Darla heard Lisbeth say as she approached the staircase.

Warmth flooded through her. *Lisbeth thinks of me as a friend.*

Through the last few months, Lisbeth had told Darla a few snippets of her story. She'd come to America on a ship from Ireland six years ago, as a maid to a wealthy lady. The woman had treated her like a pet, telling her how to dress and act and even what foods to eat. "I felt like a kitten," Lisbeth had said. She'd run off with a worthless man. After her husband drank himself to death, she'd somehow made her way to Dallas, where Ma Downs had found her in an alley, frozen to the bone. The matriarch of Downs House had, of course, brought her home, and she'd been living there for two years.

Darla felt as though the girl kept her true self locked away somewhere. Her eyes were always a little too bright, her laughter a bit too sudden.

Feeling her own eyebrows sink in concern, Darla smoothed out her forehead with gloved fingers. *I can't think about troublesome things right now.* She hurried down the stairs and out the door. *I'm going to have a splendid day. Who knows when I'll get another one?*

She rounded the corner to the barn.

There he was, leaning against the wall, wrapped in his leather duster jacket. The air had taken on a chill since morning, and Ethan's breath created a white cloud around him. He straightened as she moved closer.

Tipping his hat, he said, "I thought you weren't coming."

"And miss a day of fun? Not a chance."

He laughed and gestured for her to follow him through the gate. "I decided not to bother with the buggy; the ladies might want it. The fair's only a short distance." Sudden concern sprang into his eyes. "You don't mind, do you?"

She held back a giggle. "No, I don't like being cooped up in those rattletraps anyway. I'd much rather walk or ride. I miss Jimmy."

"Jimmy? Who's Jimmy?"

"He was my horse." She smiled at the memory of the scrawny old buckskin. "Won him in a . . ." She caught herself. "He was my horse," she repeated. "I gave him to Brother Jenkins. I didn't think there'd be room for him at Downs House."

Ethan rubbed the back of his neck. "I'm sorry you had to lose him."

"It's all right. I'm sure he's happier in the home Brother Jenkins promised to find for him. He was a cuss to ride sometimes, anyway." The words came out before she could stop them, and she slapped a hand over her mouth.

Ethan stopped. "Miss Darla, you are full of surprises. I never know what you are going to say or do next."

"I'm sorry." Darla kicked at a rock. "My dad called me his little spitfire. But I'm trying to settle down and be more proper. I really am."

Ethan turned, raised a hand and touched her cheek. The movement was so sudden she almost drew back, but caught herself and stood still, hardly daring to move. Her heart pounded like it never had, not even with such gestures from the few men who had taken her fancy in the past.

"Don't settle down too much," said Ethan softly. "I like your wildness. It makes you special. I want to know all about you. What you like the best. Where you come from."

Merry music drifted on the wind. "The fair, it must be right down the road," Darla leaned away from him.

He drew back his hand. "Yes. I'm sorry. Being forward again." Putting his hands in his pockets, he walked towards the music.

You can be forward all day long, if you like. Just don't ask so many questions. She bowed her head and followed him to the gates of the fair.

Crowds of people swarmed past like colorful ants. Boys dressed in knee-breeches and little girls in white frocks with stiff velvet bows. Housewives balancing cakes and farmers carrying vegetables and leading animals of all kinds. Barkers fought to be heard over the noise, shouting accolades for shows full of wonders that could 'be seen for just a penny. Acts seen only in the royal courts of Persia before this very day.'

Delicious scents filled the air: popcorn, roasted meat and sweets.

Darla had been to small county fairs, but nothing of this size. She clasped her hands before her, trying to see everything at once.

Ethan chuckled. "It's something, isn't it? And this is nothing compared to the state fair, but that won't come until September. I haven't been to one since . . ." His face clouded a bit. "Well, it's been awhile."

He scuffed the ground with his shoe and smiled again. "Well, what do you want to do first? Are you hungry?"

"No, not at all," Darla said as her stomach growled. She swallowed and pressed her arms against her midsection.

"Of course you are. That cabbage soup we had for lunch couldn't keep a fly alive." Ethan grimaced. "Ma does insist on serving it once a week for the digestion." He took her hand and pulled her towards a food stall.

The gesture was quick and innocent enough, but Darla fought the temptation to snatch her hand back lest her train of thought be somehow transferred through touch. *What does this mean? Should I allow him to hold my hand? If I let go now, it would be terribly rude, and he wouldn't understand. I truly care for him. Yes.* She closed her eyes. *Yes I do. Oh dear, I've tried so hard not to!*

Good thing Ethan's attention was focused on the food booths. If he had looked back, he would have seen a conflicting display of emotions parade across her face while her mind sorted through these thoughts. As it was, she drew curious expressions from several of the people passing by.

At one booth, a woman was frying doughnuts in an iron skillet of bubbling grease. When the dough was fried, she'd flip it onto a stack at one end of the booth. On the other side of the counter was a skillet for frying chicken.

"Doughnut and chicken for a nickel!" she called to Ethan in a voice that was more like a song than a speech.

"I think that's just what we're looking for," Ethan said. Before Darla could fumble in her reticule for one of her precious coins, he pulled out a shiny dime and set it on the counter. "May I have two of each, please?"

"Oh, Ethan, I couldn't ask you to!" Darla protested.

"You didn't." He let go of her hand to take his chicken and doughnut.

She took her food as well. The doughnut was soft and warm in one hand, the chicken crisp and hot in the other.

Ethan looked around. "I don't see any places to sit, and the ground is pretty muddy here. We'll have to stand and eat. Do you mind?"

"Not at all."

After eating every crumb and licking their fingers in scandalous abandon, they continued through the fair. Sword swallowers and jugglers performed in front of bright tents, and women danced through the crowd in low-cut dresses with colored spangles. Whenever one of these performers came too close to Ethan he'd turn away with flaming cheeks.

Darla's head swam when she remembered only months before she'd go out in public every day wearing much less. *How could I have been so shameless?*

Ethan nudged her gently. "What's the matter? Aren't you having a good time?"

"The very best." But tiny fingers of doubt began to poke and prod at her heart. *He couldn't care for me if he knew.* She wished she could just forget, to throw these thoughts from her mind and enjoy the day--her day--with her dashing young gentleman.

"Why, I declare, it's Ethan Downs!" A woman's voice, rather high and shrill despite the Texas drawl, pierced through the crowd.

Darla sighed. Samantha Bugle. *And the afternoon was going so well.*

Samantha floated up to Ethan in a flouncing silk dress with a gigantic bustle. A hat, drooping with enough feathers to make up a whole bird, kept impossible balance on her gleaming brown tresses.

She shook Ethan's hand, giving Darla a slit-eyed glare over his shoulder. "Ethan, look at how sweet you are! Showing kindness to an unfortunate, even on your day off."

"Er, that's not really--" Ethan began.

Samantha interrupted. "But of course you're the kindest man in all of Dallas, aren't you?" She turned to Darla. "And dear, you wouldn't mind if I took him away for a bit?" She gave Ethan a doe-eyed look. "Papa needs help, and I promised him I'd find a strong young man to help unload his prized steer at the judging pens."

Darla's hackles rose. She was tempted to rip the ridiculous hat off those curls and stomp it to the ground. Instead, she gave her sweetest honey-fake smile, the one that she used to reserve for her dullest customers.

"You go right on ahead. I'm going to stroll over and listen to the band." She gave Ethan a sideways glance. "Maybe one of those fellows over there will take pity on a poor girl and ask me to dance."

The tips of Ethan's ears turned red. "Miss Bugle, I don't want to leave Miss North alone."

Samantha pouted and batted her long, thick lashes. "Can't you spare a moment for a dear, dear family friend? It's practically an emergency."

Emergency, my eye. It's probably a tiny calf I could carry out by myself. But Darla shrugged. "Go on, find out what all this fuss is about. I can amuse myself for a few moments."

Ethan squeezed her hand. "I'll be right back. I promise."

10

A Dangerous Dance

Darla refused to watch as Samantha dragged Ethan away through the crowd. She didn't want to give the woman the satisfaction.

Scooting closer to the music, she craned her neck to see the band through the crowd.

One man with a thick moustache and a bright vest played an accordion, while another strummed a guitar. An older fellow with gray in his hair held a violin. A beautiful woman with dark hair flowing down her back beat a tambourine against a slender wrist. The music was mysterious and joyful at the same time, with notes and chords Darla had never heard.

A cowboy with a thick blond beard approached her and offered his arm. Darla needed no further encouragement. She followed his steps into the whirling, swirling dance.

The tempo quickened, and a different man traded places with the cowboy. He was replaced with a third, and then a fourth.

The simple steps were easy to follow, and Darla threw herself into then. Freedom bubbled up within her. *It's been so long since I could be me. Just Darla.*

"Darla?" The fifth man stopped short, jerking her to a halt. "Well, ain't you a sight for sore eyes? What the Sam Hill are you doing down here in Dallas, anyway?"

Red hair stood up on the man's pale head like stubble in a harvested wheat field. His cheeks were crimson and round, and his thick lips were flecked with spittle.

Darla stepped back. "You must be mistaken, sir. My name is . . . Lisbeth."

"No, no it ain't." The man grabbed at her hand. She pushed further away, almost stumbling into the couples still dancing around them. *Jethro Sites. But how did he end up in Dallas?* "Please, just let me be!"

The man stomped after her, his eyes lit up like two coals in a scuttle. "Honey, come on. You and I had a good time at that ol' saloon, didn't we? I liked your dancing and singing better'n any of the other gals. I always gave you an extra coin or two when I had one." He leaned closer, and a stream of hot, stagnant breath hit her face. "Come on to the whiskey stand and we'll have some fun, like we used to."

The thought of whiskey made Darla's throat burn. She'd never cared for the stuff, though she'd been forced to drink it a few times. She scanned the crowd, searching for Ethan. *Where is he?*

Step by step, she backed out of the circle.

Jethro's eyes drooped like a sad puppy. "C'mon, what's the matter?"

"Leave me alone!" She was almost to the edge of the crowd. Once past the dancers, she picked up her skirts and ran, weaving through the booths and tents.

Venders leaned against their carts, wide-eyed. Crowds parted, most probably thinking she was part of an act.

After a distance, Darla leaned against a wagon of brilliant gold with carved cherubs on the sides. Gasping for breath, she peeked around the corner. No Jethro.

"Pardon, Miss, can I help you with something?"

Pressing fingers against her lips to hold back a yelp, she turned to see a boy with tangled blond hair staring up at her.

His clothes were fashioned of tattered but costly material, and his shoes, Darla noticed with interest, had bells on the pointed tips.

'I know. Dandy, ain't they?" He wiggled his foot and smiled at the jingle.

"Shhhh . . ." She peered out into the fair once more. *What if Jethro finds me? What if Ethan sees him and finds out who I was?*

The thought was so chilling her knees wobbled.

The boy's face grew solemn. "You seem to be in trouble, Miss."

"I suppose I am," Darla admitted.

His eyes widened. "Ain't you pretty, though? I thought pretty girls could talk their way outta any kind of problem."

Darla gave him a wry smile. "If only."

"If you want some help, Doctor Ebenezer might be able to do something. He takes care a' all of us."

"All of you?" Darla glanced around, but saw no one else near the wagon.

The boy pointed to the cart's side.

"Dr. Ebenezer's Traveling Medical Show of Wonders," Darla read out loud.

The lad's chest puffed with pride. "Yep. And we're the very best. We got zanies, a snake charmer, and Lucy, of course."

"Who's Lucy?"

"The smartest, most trained pig you ever saw. And the gypsies, of course."

Now Darla could hear it. Music grew louder, nearing her hiding place. She peeked out to see the musicians leading a parade of folks up the lane, right towards the wagon.

Behind them walked Ethan. Was he shouting her name? Her fingers tightened around a wooden curlicue.

The boy must have noticed her relieved expression. He leaned closer. "Is everything all right now, ma'am?"

She nodded and stood up, smoothing her skirts.

He tugged on her sleeve. "Miss, if you ever decide you need some help after all, come to the fairgrounds and ask for Johnny Jingle. We'll be here for two more days. Dr. Ebenezer would be pleased as punch to have a purty girl like you join the troupe, and we have lots of fun."

"Thanks, Sugar." Darla reached out to pat the tousled head, saw a few crawling specks in the blond strands, and drew her hand back. "Good luck to you and your show."

She ran out from behind the wagon and called, "Ethan! I'm over here!"

Ethan trotted over, his eyebrows drawn together. "Darla, where were you? I thought you might have been kidnapped by a vagrant magician."

She managed a laugh. "No, silly. I got tired of the music and went for a walk. When I saw this wagon, I just had to get a closer look. Wouldn't it be fun to travel with a medicine show?"

Ethan surveyed the golden carvings and frowned. "Take up with a snake oil salesman? All they do is cheat folks out of hard-earned money." His features softened. "I never know what you're going to think of next. Why did you run off like that? I was worried about you."

"Sorry." Darla lowered her head, and then looked up with a saucy smile. "But what's a girl to do when left all on her own?"

"You're right." Ethan sighed. "I shouldn't have gone off with that Samantha Bugle. After I helped with the steer, she wanted me to help unload her mother's pumpkins. I don't mind helping the benefactors but . . ." He scowled. "Sometimes, that woman . . ."

Darla remained silent, but her heart leapt at the exasperated look on his face. Up until now she'd wondered if Ethan might care for Samantha a tiny bit, but now his true feelings were obvious.

Ethan tugged her shoulder gently so she turned to face him. "Hey. I'll forgive you for disappearing on me if you'll forgive me for leaving you all alone."

"I can do that," Darla replied.

Bending close to her ear, Ethan whispered, "Just don't run off on me again. Please?"

"I promise," she whispered back.

Over Ethan's shoulder, Jethro's red face appeared once more, shining like a beacon through the crowd. Her heart sank. She'd almost forgotten the reason she'd run off in the first place.

She whipped around and walked in quick steps toward the front gates. "Ethan, we should be heading back, don't you think? Your Ma might need you and wonder why we're both gone."

Ethan's mouth drew down at the corners. "Ma knows I need my own time. She won't be worrying about me."

Darla chose not to argue that point. She glanced behind her. No Jethro. *Maybe he didn't see me.* Giving a weak smile, she pulled her shawl tighter around her shoulders. "I'm getting a bit cold and I don't want to catch the sniffles. I'm sorry to spoil the day, but I probably should go home."

"It has become more brisk, hasn't it? All right then." Ethan's forehead creased. "I would have enjoyed a dance."

He looked so much like a pouting little boy that Darla had to laugh. "Next time," she promised.

As they rounded the gate and started down the road, she listened for the sound of feet scuffling behind them. No one. Breathing a sigh of relief, she wrapped her fingers around Ethan's arm.

"Is everything all right?" He glanced down at her. "Please don't fret about Ma. She gets in a frazzle about money and the benefactors and the state of the house. I keep telling her to trust in God, but she worries still. If she's out of sorts, it's because of all the other things."

I'm sure she'd be even more 'out of sorts' if she knew her son had taken an unfortunate to the fair. I'd bet she'd have a fit of vapors if she found out I was a former saloon girl.

As they reached home, Darla pressed her fingers against her forehead. "I'm feeling a bit tired. I think I'll go lie down in my room until supper."

"You aren't ill, are you?"

No, no. I'm fine." She patted his arm. "I had a really nice time today. At least until Samantha Bugle came along."

Ethan's lips curled into a slow smile. "Don't be too mean. After all, she is a dear family friend."

He reached over, faster than she could blink, and gave her a quick kiss on the cheek. Then he strode through the front gate and off to the direction of the barn.

Her fingers caressed the place where the kiss had fallen. On to the house she went, fighting the urge to skip up the front steps like a little girl.

11

A Fateful Night

"Home already?"

Darla's fingers stopped, stretched towards the banister. She pulled them back and put her hands in her pockets. "Yes, ma'am." She turned to face Ma Downs. "I was feeling a bit chilled." *Oh dear. She must have found out about Ethan taking me to the fair. This is it. She'll ask me to leave for sure.* A glimpse of her own reflection in a mirror over the woman's shoulder showed her white, frightened face.

"Darla, will you please come into my study?"

She bowed her head and followed Ma Downs into the small room, complete with bookshelves stuffed with books and a roll-top desk with mountains of papers.

Ma Downs indicated a chair. "I wanted to discuss something with you."

Sitting down hard, Darla held still, hardly daring to breathe.

The feathers on the eternal black hat drooped almost to the desk as Ma Downs bent to look at a paper. "I've had so many letters to write. Patrons tend to forget their promises in the winter months." She glanced up, frowning. "My father never begged for help, no matter how lean it got. Many times, I saw my breakfast ride away in the back of the poor folk's wagon. My father always said we'd have treasures in Heaven. But that's a hard thing for a five-year-old to understand when hunger's gnawing at her belly."

Darla inhaled sharply, but didn't reply. *Ma Downs wasn't lying when she said she's had her share of tough times.*

"My father was too proud to ask for help, and my mother was too proud to sell any of the furniture or art from our family home. In the end, I've had to do both, and I don't regret either."

Confusion pooled in Darla's mind. *If she's asking me to leave, why can't she get to it?* She squirmed in her chair.

"Providing help to women in need has been the most rewarding part of my life, besides raising my boys. Darla, I am happy to tell you your trial at Downs House is finished. You have proven to be a hard worker, and I see you truly want to follow God's will, even though there might be some hiccups along the way. You may stay here as long as you wish."

Unable to stop the gusty sigh of relief, Darla sank back into her chair. "Thank you so much. I'll do my best to make you proud."

Ma Downs held out a gloved hand. "I'm sure you will." She stared deep into Darla's eyes. "Don't break his heart, Darla."

Even as Darla grasped the woman's hand, a thought sped through her mind like a Texas tornado. *This is the moment. I've got to make sure she knows about my past.* But her lips stuck together, and the words would not come. She stood up and left the room, feeling as though Ma Downs's eyes might bore into her soul.

Darla didn't see Ethan until after supper when she went outside to finish up the evening chores. His work boots stuck from under the wall beneath the kitchen window. When she peeked under the boards she saw one hand draped across his mid-section. The other was somewhere up under the floor, employing a hammer for some repair.

What strong, capable hands. A tiny sigh escaped Darla's lips.

Ethan scooted out and sat up, dirt and bits of grass sticking to his hair and face. "Hey there. Feeling better?" He looked her over, as though checking for signs of impending ailments.

"Oh yes, much." She smoothed her skirts and bent down to peer under the house. "What are you working on?"

Reaching under the crawl space, Ethan pulled out a lantern. "These floor joists are almost rotted through in places. Very unsafe. I need to replace them somehow, but large pieces of timber are expensive. It might be even worse towards the center of the house, but I'd have to pull up the floor to find out."

He stood up, brushing off his clothes. "We don't have any extra funds to spare right now. Even if I did all the work myself, we couldn't afford the lumber."

"What about the benefactors?" asked Darla, picking a tiny leaf from Ethan's sleeve.

"Ma sent out more letters, but she isn't expecting much. Times are tight right now, even for rich folks."

"Weren't you just saying we need to stop worrying and trust in God?" Darla said. "Didn't Reverend Martin say we should pray without ceasing last week?"

Ethan nodded. "You're right, Darla, I need to listen to my own advice."

"Things will work out, you just wait and see." The giddy sensation brought on by Ma's earlier announcement still filled Darla's head. "I'd better get going. I was on my way to close up the chicken coop. See you in the morning." Darla flounced off in the direction of the barn.

She poked her head inside the small, triangle-shaped building to make sure the hens were all in for the night. Settled bundles of feathers poked out from nesting boxes.

After latching the door, Darla went to the gazebo, which had become her regular place to pray and think. She sank down on the wooden bench, listening to the coos and clucks through the coop wall while the chickens said their goodnights.

Closing her eyes, she imagined herself back on her dad's farm. Her mother had passed away when she was three. Since her father had little time for anything but the farm, he'd dressed her in overalls and cut her hair short to keep away bugs. She had followed him everywhere. *I would have been there still, if he hadn't died. We'd be running the farm together.* She brushed away a sudden tear. Difficult as chores had been these past few months, they held unexpected joy. Every smell and sound brought back memories of a safe home and her loving father.

She left the gazebo, but paused when she passed the coop door. "Good night, you crazy biddies."

"Darla?" a rough voice called from the street.

"Jethro?" Darla's lips trembled so much she could barely form the words. "What are you doing here?"

Trees sent jagged shadows over the front gate where Jethro stood. "Hey, girl, I tracked you down! Couldn't let a pretty thing like you slip through the cracks." He tipped his hat back and grinned. "What are you doing in a dismal place like this, anyhow?" His words slurred, and he struggled to focus on her face.

"You should get to wherever you're staying and sleep off that whiskey." Her eyes darted around the yard, checking for members of the house. "Please leave me alone. I don't want to speak to you."

"Come on, sweetie." Jethro leaned over the rough wooden slats. "I'll show you a good time. I know you missed me."

"Go away," Darla hissed. "I left that life behind and I'm not going back."

"What? Darla, you were the purtiest girl in the saloon. The fellows talk about you all the time."

Rocks crunched behind her, and Ethan moved to her side. Her shoulders sagged in relief. "Oh, Ethan. Please make him leave."

"You heard the lady." Ethan stepped in front of her, and the muscles in his jaw twitched. "This is a safe house. Move on now."

Jethro gave a short laugh. "Wasn't long ago, this girl asked for me, special. She always picked me to dance the hurdy-gurdies. Don't you remember, Darla?"

Ethan inhaled sharply. "Darla, you know this man?"

Darla could bear it no longer. Clapping her hands over her face, she ran to the porch, through the door and up the stairs to her room. Lisbeth hadn't come up yet. *Where is she? I'm surprised everyone's not outside hearing my life story from Jethro by now.*

Rushing to the window, she peeked at the two men, still staring each other down in the moonlight. Her breaths came in ragged gasps that fogged up the pane. She wiped it with her sleeve.

The cowboy's face had turned red. He was shouting something at Ethan, who looked ready to jump over the gate. Darla wished with all her heart she could open the window and hear what was being said, but the wooden frames stuck terribly, and would be sure to make noise loud enough for them to hear.

A loud blast echoed through the walls. Ethan and Jethro both ducked down.

Ma Downs appeared out by the gate, holding a shotgun.

Jethro stood up slowly, his hands above his head. After he shouted something else Darla still couldn't hear, he turned on his heel and walked away.

Ethan and Ma Downs leaned over the gate and watched after him. After a long time, Ma Downs lowered the gun, and they both turned to look up at Darla's window.

She gasped and moved away from the curtains.

What can I do, what can I do? Jethro must have told them. Her knees buckled, and she sat down hard on the bed. *Well, that's it. Tomorrow I'll be thrown out of Downs House once and for all.*

She bit her lip until it stung. Getting thrown out of the house, she could endure. Ma's disappointment would be hard to see, but she could handle it. The ladies would feel betrayed. But . . . *Ethan.* She couldn't bear to picture the look on his face as she left in disgrace.

Darla girl, time to think. She glanced at the door. Lisbeth would be up to bed any time now.

The wagon she'd hid behind at the fair popped into her mind. Doctor Ebenezer's Medical Marvels. *That young boy was pretty convinced they'd take me on. Maybe I could clean the wagons for them or something. At least I wouldn't starve.*

Darla pulled off her shoes and washed her face. Instead of putting on a nightgown, she changed into a day dress. She chose one she'd purchased, not one provided by Down's House. She packed her few possessions in her carpet bag and shoved them under the bed.

A hot tear slid down her cheek as she got under the covers and pulled them tightly under her chin. *How could you think you'd make it here? You don't deserve such a place, not after what you've done.* Even as the harsh words grated on her mind, she knew they weren't true. But she allowed them to flood through her anyway. Hope couldn't have a place in her heart any longer. *It hurts too much.*

A few minutes later, Lisbeth came into the room. "Darla?"

Darla closed her eyes and tried to breathe evenly.

"Danny, I guess Darla's asleep," she heard Lisbeth whisper. 'Goodness, I don't know how she could have slept through that ruckus! Ma Downs must have thought that man was dangerous."

Darla lay quietly, waiting for what seemed like years, until she heard her friend's gentle snores. *I have to leave. What if Jethro comes back? I can't bring danger to this place. These people are good and kind. They don't need that.*

She got out of bed and stared at the sleeping woman. Danny was curled in Lisbeth's hair, fluffy brown fur mixed in the red strands.

I'll miss you all so much. How can I bear it! Blinking away tears, she pulled on her socks and shoes, grabbed her carpet bag, and crept down the stairs and into the night.

Part 2
Passage

12

The Gates

Trees on both sides of the road leaned out toward Darla as she made her way down the lane. Brilliant light shone from the moon and stars, reminding her of the night a few months ago when she'd galloped away from her old life. It seemed fitting for this evening to be so similar. The flitting shadows led the way, as vague and shapeless as her future.

When Darla reached the fairground entrance, it appeared to be deserted. The gates stood with beams crossed in defiance to anyone who dared try and invade them. The patient moon shone down as if to say, "I lit the way. That's the best I could do."

What am I doing here? There's no guarantee the medicine show will take me on. It's more likely I'll get hauled off to jail. Darla twisted a curl around her finger. Which would be worse, explaining her past to Ma Downs, or facing a judge? *I'd rather go to jail. As long as Ethan doesn't find out where I am.*

A glow from the left caught her eye. As she crept closer to the light, she saw a lumpy tent pitched to the far side of the gate, half-hidden in the brush. The spicy, choking scent of a cheap cigar drifted through the night. A few glowing embers in a pit lay before her. The light must be coming from a lantern, which meant the guard was probably sitting on the other side of the tent.

Of course there's a guard. Darla tiptoed back to the gates and examined them in the moonlight. The bars weren't secured by a lock, but with thick lengths of rope, twisted into complicated knots.

In her various professions Darla had dealt with her share of knots, but the dim light made progress difficult. She wished she hadn't been so quick to relinquish her dagger and pistol. She poked and prodded at the rope until her fingers stung from the coarse fibers. *Lord, please help me get inside.*

In her frustration, she jostled the gate and the boards protested with a loud creak.

The tent moved, and a lantern swung around the side of the tent.

Darla jumped back, blinking in the sudden light.

"Hey lady, what are you doing out here in the middle of the night?" The guard was stocky and squat, with a bushy beard that cascaded down his chest like Spanish moss.

"Oh, thank goodness you're here, sir." Darla smiled her sweetest smile. "I need to get inside, please." She allowed her lip to tremble.

The guard gave her a wary glance-over. "Hmph. I'm not supposed to let anyone in the gate after ten of the clock." He fumbled in his pocket, pulled out a watch and peered at it in the lantern light. "It's now half past eleven. So you'll just have to wait until the morning light of dawn, ma'am."

"Oh please, please let me in." Darla clasped her hands in front of her. Sudden inspiration struck. "My daddy will kill me dead if he knows I'm out here."

The guard's thick eyebrows lifted. "What do you mean? And if you belong with someone in there, why do you have that?" He pointed to her traveling bag.

A blink or two, and a few tears squeezed from Darla's eyes and coursed down her cheeks. She gazed towards the heavens. "Oh, I've been awful. You see, I met Harry last week on the first night of the fair. He gave me all this sweet talk and won me a prize from the strong man contest! But Daddy didn't like him one bit. Daddy calls the square dances." She stole a glance at the guard, who was listening with his mouth hanging open.

"Anyways, Harry asked me to run away with him, and I packed up all my worldly goods." She held up her bag. "And took off like a wicked, evil girl. Can you imagine, good sir? After all my daddy has done for me, raising me like I was his very own?"

The guard blinked. "Wasn't you his own?"

"Of course I was—am," said Darla in haste. "But you wouldn't think it the way I've treated him, now would you?"

To her satisfaction, another, much larger tear slid down her cheek. In the past those tears had bought her money, jewelry, and even a pet poodle, which she'd sold to a small town widow for fifty cents.

The tears did not lose their power with the bearded man. Reaching a meaty paw into his pocket, he brought out a surprisingly clean handkerchief and handed it to her.

"Don't fret there, miss. Maybe your Pa'll forgive you when you show up in the morning."

"You don't understand." Darla batted her now tear-fringed eyelashes. "I must get back before dawn. If he wakes up to find me missing, why, he might just fall down in a fit. He's had them before. In San Antone," she added for good measure.

She wiped her eyes a final time and handed the handkerchief back to the guard.

He folded it carefully and placed it back in his pocket. "Well, if it's life and death like you say . . ." He shuffled to the gate.

Even through her elation Darla could feel the lies burning the back of her throat. *I'm sorry, God.* A bit shocked by how easily they still came, she pressed a hand against her forehead. *Well, I can't back out now. I have no choice.*

"No choice?" A still small voice spoke. *"Is this a choice I've set before you?"*

Darla glanced over her shoulder, though she knew the whisper had come from inside. *Surely that can't be God. Why would He choose to speak to me now?* After that day on the street by the Dallas saloon, she'd longed to hear the voice of God once more. But now she doubted He'd give her the time of day after the flurry of untruths that had poured from her mouth.

Before she could decide what to do, the guard had finished untying his mysterious set of knots.

He swung the gate open and nodded to her.

"Wait," said Darla, "I need to tell you . . ."

Rattling wheels interrupted her would-be confession as a caravan of gilded wagons paraded towards the gate. Lanterns hanging from the fronts of the wagons bobbed like ghostly beacons in the night.

A slight, thin boy with hay-like blond hair appeared in the door of the wagon that was second in line. He rushed to Darla, the bells on his shoes jingling with every step.

"Oh, Darla, what are you doing out here?" He winked and grabbed her hand, tugging her past the guard's astonished face. "You shouldn't be wandering off during one of your crazy spells."

The guard pushed back his hat. "You mean this girl's with your outfit?"

A very short, very bald man with a handlebar moustache peered over the driver's seat of the first wagon. He stared at Darla for a moment, nodded and jumped down from his perch. "That she is, good sir." He shook the guard's hand. "Doctor Ebenezer, at your service."

He stepped up to Darla and sighed. "This woman does suffer from some mild ailments, but I can cure every fit of insanity."

"Wait . . . which one has fits?" The guard turned to Darla. "I thought he had fits?"

Doctor Ebenezer held up a hand. "Sir, I must be on hand every morning to give her this patent blend I created myself, from the honey of Canadian bees." He pulled a small bottle from his pocket, along with a tiny silver spoon. Uncorking the bottle, he drizzled a bit of liquid into the spoon.

Both Darla and the guard watched in fascination.

"There, take your medicine like a good girl." He held the spoon out to Darla, his gnarled, mottled hand shaking a bit. He must have noticed the uncertainty in her face, because he winked.

Darla squeezed her eyes shut and downed the spoonful in a hurry. The concoction was a bit thick on the tongue, but not unpleasant.

Doctor Ebenezer smiled. "Good girl. Feel better?"

"I feel . . ." A few words from the label caught her eye in the lantern-light. "Fresh and full of vitality."

"Come on, Darla, we'd better get in the wagon." Johnny Jingles tugged on her hand.

As Darla followed him, she heard the guard speaking to the doctor. "I'm glad you came along. I didn't quite know what to think of her."

"Yes, yes, quite sorry," the doctor said. "She's always been a bit of a tangle, that one. Takes after her mother, I suppose. If you have no objection, we'll be off. The fair manager knows we decided to leave tonight, all is squared away."

The doctor took Darla's hand. "Hop on board, my dear, and we'll be on our way."

A strong scent of animals and leather surrounded Darla as she entered the wagon, and a muffled snort came from the corner of the large, box-like area. The room inside was as wide and long as a small house, larger than any contained wagon she'd seen.

Johnny came in, hung a lantern on the wall, and closed the door. Though he couldn't have been older than twelve, he wore the smile of a wise old man. Darla recognized the look, worn by every orphan from the children's home where she had grown up, the same expression she saw on her own face every time she glanced in a mirror.

A glint in his eye belied a likable and fun-loving spirit. "You'd better sit down, Miss Darla. These wagons jolt a bit, 'specially when the roads are muddy."

Darla perched on a low bench built into the wall, and none too soon. The wagon jerked forward and would have sent her tumbling.

Objects around her began to take shape as her eyes adjusted to the semi-darkness.

The box-like things built into the left wall were wooden crates, and the lump swinging from the ceiling was a wire bird cage. The most unusual bird Darla had ever seen, with feathers of green, blue and yellow, stared at her with a sleepy eye.

She couldn't see the end of the wagon the snort had come from, but she assumed other types of beasts were kept over there.

"Excuse me, Miss Darla," Johnny said. "You did come to the fairgrounds because you'd changed your mind, right. I told Doctor Ebenezer about you, that's why he covered for you with the guard."

"Yes, there is nothing in Dallas for me now," she said, realizing how dramatic the words must sound. "If I could earn a ride to the next town, I'd be awfully grateful."

"You'll have to talk that over with Doctor Ebenezer." Johnny reached up to cover the bird's cage with a large cloth and then settled on the bench beside her. "But we lost a sales girl a few stops back, so the doc'll probably be glad to have you." He gave her a slanted look. "If you want to stay."

"The doctor seems very kind,' Darla murmured.

Johnny nodded, his forehead wrinkling. "He's not a bad sort. Sometimes he gets moody, though. Like tonight, he up and decided to leave the fair, when sales had been pretty good. He didn't tell anyone why. Sometimes he just has these hunches. We go along with what he says. It's saved us from ticklish times, I can tell you that." The boy wriggled his shoulders and settled against the wall.

"I wonder what he'll ask me to do," Darla mused. "I wouldn't want to do anything morally objectionable."

Johnny jerked forward. "Naw, we aren't like that here. You'll see. The last girl just walked through the crowd to show things. Bottles and stuff. Handed out papers with information to folks who could read." He studied her face. "Doctor Ebenezer might ask you to sing something. Can you sing?"

"I can sing." Darla folded her arms in front of her.

"So's your mother would listen, or for a crowd?"

"For a crowd, silly."

Johnny stood and walked over to one of the cages, as at home with the swaying wagon as a sailor on his ship. He peered in and poked at something. "Good. Shirley's eaten her rat. The last thing I needed was for the thing to gnaw through the bars." He looked over at Darla. "Don't worry. We'll be stopping in less than an hour, soon as we find a camping spot. You won't have to sleep in here with the snakes." He sat down again.

Snakes? Darla had never been timid about creepy-crawlies, but if a snake were to fall on her head it would be rather unsettling. She eyed the cages and drew her skirts closer around her feet.

True to Johnny's word, it wasn't long before the wagons came to a halt.

The boy's head snapped up. "See? What did I tell you? We could stay in the wagons, and sometimes everyone will on the coldest nights. But it's pretty warm for March. So we'll sleep in tents tonight."

He grabbed the lantern and went from cage to cage, murmuring a few words to each animal. Seemingly satisfied, he moved to the wagon door and swung it open. "Come on, I'll introduce you to the rest of the folks."

Darla stood in haste, bumping her head on the bird cage. An indignant squawk came from underneath the cloth.

"Ooohh . . ." She rubbed her head, picked up her carpet bag, and stepped outside.

In the five years since she'd been sent from the orphanage at seventeen to 'find her own way,' Darla had worked as a maid, cook and cleaning woman, including one memorable morning as a nursemaid to a crotchety old man who smelled of cabbage and called her "Twinkle Toes." She'd been hired by three saloon owners who'd all possessed their own kind of crazy. But though her life had been a parade of meetings with colorful folks, nothing prepared her for the group of people setting up camp outside the wagon door.

The gypsy men, still dressed in dazzling outfits, bustled about throwing armloads of wood in a pile. A gypsy woman led two little boys to log seats and sat down herself, arranging a baby over her lap to nurse.

One man bent to light the fire. Soon flames leapt into the air, higher and higher, casting light on all the workers.

Two very tall, thin fellows with identical features and outfits juggled china plates beneath a clump of trees.

A woman wearing a plain gray dress, with thick dark braids piled on her head and skin so white it glowed in the semi-darkness, lugged a giant kettle from the back of the third wagon.

Darla's mouth dropped open. "How did they get everything prepared so quickly?" she asked Johnny, who was examining the side of the wagon.

"We'd already cooked supper before we left, but the doctor was jumpy and no one got to eat. They packed it up and we moved on," Johnny explained. He sauntered over to the woman in gray, who was now ladling stew from the pot. "Hey, Miss Miranda, could you get a bowl for the new girl, here?" He jabbed a thumb at Darla.

"Pleased to meet you, I'm sure." Miss Miranda's eyes never left her work as she filled a rough wooden trencher and handed it to Darla. Pale as she was, the woman possessed a cold beauty. She seemed to be in her early thirties.

"Thank you." Darla stood with her fingers curled around the bowl. The woman didn't look up. Realizing the conversation was complete, Darla followed Johnny to the fire.

On the way, Johnny stopped to watch the two jugglers.

"Darla, this is Simon and Aaron Henderson. We call them the zanies. They used to be clowns in a real circus."

The two men each caught their respective plates, turned and tipped their hats as one, almost as though they were a mirror image of the same person.

"Evening ma'am," they said in unison.

A beautiful gypsy girl with long, brown tresses tied back in a colorful scarf used a wooden rake to clear the ground on the side of the campfire.

Johnny stopped in front of her. "Ketzia, meet Darla."

Ketzia leaned the wooden rake she'd been using against a tree and held out her hand. Golden bracelets hanging from her elbow to her wrist jangled with the movement. "Hello. Welcome to the medicine show," she said warmly. Her words were clipped by a slight accent Darla did not recognize.

"Thank you." Darla shook her offered hand.

Ketzia nodded to Johnny. "Four days."

"Take you up," said Johnny. Pulling a coin from his pocket, he flipped it in the air.

Ketzia caught it and hid it somewhere in her shawl.

Darla knew when a bet was being placed. "What was that all about?" she asked Johnny as they finally settled by the fire with their stew.

"Oh, don't pay it no mind. Ketzia and I always make bets about how long the new folks'll stay."

"Oh." Darla took a bite of stew. She'd made her share of wagers, but wasn't sure if she appreciated being the subject of a bet.

After Darla was finished eating, she helped Johnny and Ketzia pitch tents and spread out blankets inside. But the lack of a normal bedtime was taking its toll, and she kept yawning and rubbing her eyes.

Finally, all was ready and Johnny led her back to Miss Miranda.

"You'll sleep in my tent for now," said the woman.

"Oh, thank you." Darla's shoulders grew limp with relief. As tired as she was, she wouldn't have slept a wink in the snake wagon.

The tent was well made, and surprisingly spacious. Miss Miranda pointed to a pallet, already made up with thick flannel blankets. "That's your space, over there."

For Darla, sleep was a long time coming. Every time she closed her eyes, she thought of someone else she'd left behind, someone who would think badly of her in the morning. Tears streamed from her eyes onto the small, flat pillow, but she choked back her sobs. She didn't want to disturb Miss Miranda.

Finally, the trembling hand of sleep found it's place, and she floated away to a world of darkened dreams.

ANGELA CASTILLO

13

The Troupe

The next morning, Ethan came into the kitchen. He whistled while he washed his hands. Swiping a cinnamon bun from Mrs. Betty--somehow they always tasted better when stolen--he headed to the dining room with a spring in his step.

I can't wait to see her. Even though he'd spent most of the night staring at the ceiling with wide eyes, a fresh, new energy coursed through his veins. He hadn't felt this way since . . . since before Sarah left him. *Sarah.* The name had lost the power to stab with its usual white-hot needle of pain and regret. Finally, these feelings had faded to a hazy memory. *I can move past that now.* He'd known for a long time that God had forgiven him for the anger he'd felt during that time. *And now I can truly forgive myself.* A deep, contented sigh rose from his innermost being.

The man from last night flickered into his mind. *Wonder how that fellow found Darla? That must be why she was so upset at the fair.* He shrugged. *Maybe she'll explain sometime. I'll give her time.*

Ethan sauntered into the dining room and stooped to kiss his mother on the cheek.

"Good morning, all," he addressed the ladies. His eyes swiveled to Darla's seat. Empty. *Was she too ill for breakfast?* He stared at her vacant chair.

Lisbeth met his gaze with flashing eyes. "She's gone," she said softly. "Took all her things and ran off in the night."

A dull throb began at the back of Ethan's head. He staggered to his chair and sat down hard. "I don't understand. Where . . . did she say where she was going?"

Lisbeth held up a scrap of paper. "She left this note for the house. It says thanks for everything . . . but something happened and she couldn't stay. The note says we would know why, but I'm so confused. I can't imagine what made her want to leave. Do you know, Ethan?"

Ethan shook his head. "I have no idea. That strange fellow came by last night, but I told him to leave. Darla did seem pretty upset, but I thought she'd be all right since we chased him off."

Ma Downs sighed. "I thought Miss North was doing so well. But we have seen many ladies scared away by harmful men from their past, or tempted by wanderlust. Let us include her safety and well-being in our prayers. We will ask God to walk beside her wherever she goes."

Lisbeth blinked hard, her lips trembling. The Pendell twins sobbed into their oatmeal.

Ethan closed his eyes during the prayer and did not look up until long after dishes clattered around him from food being passed. After choking down a few bites, he excused himself from the table.

Cows lifted their heads as he crossed the field to his little cabin in the back pasture. He grabbed his fiddle from the mantle and lifted the instrument to his shoulder. Music could comfort him like nothing else, but this time only dark, harsh notes came from the ancient strings.

He set the instrument down. "God, I don't know what to think. Why would she leave? Why wouldn't she at least tell me? What if she's in danger?" *Why did you allow this to happen to me again?* He covered his face with his hands.

Remember last time. He reached into his duster pocket to touch a crumpled paper, always there. A resolution settled into his mind. *I will find her. I have to find out the reason she left.*

The light of dawn had settled like a filmy gray scarf over the trees when Darla stumbled from the tent. She had grown accustomed to early hours at Downs House, but after the late bedtime her head ached and her eyes stung. At the sight of the mirrored sconces on the sides of the lead wagon she turned her head away. She had no desire to see the state of her hair.

Stifling a yawn, Darla surveyed the camp. Most evidence of last night's activities had already been whisked away to mysterious storage places in the wagons.

Doctor Ebenezer sat by the dying coals of the morning fire, spectacles balanced on the end of his bulbous nose. He looked up from the thick book in his hands. "Good morning, Miss North."

"Good morning, Doctor," Darla said in a bright tone that she hoped sounded less frazzled than she must appear. "I wanted to thank you again for rescuing me last evening."

"Quite fine." He leapt to his feet. "Now, I want to make something perfectly clear right now, before anything is decided." Though he had to tilt his head back to look her in the eye, he carried an air of one who was accustomed to being respected and obeyed. "You are welcome to travel with this group for as long as you wish. I ask only one thing. We may have stretched the truth a bit to help you along, but my dear," he took her hand in a firm grip, "you must never betray my trust."

She shook his hand. "I hope I never lie again. Don't like how it settles in my belly."

A twinkle reached his eye and his lips twitched into a smile. "And how would I know if you were lying to me now, child?" His laughter rang out over the campground.

Darla couldn't help but join in.

Doctor Ebenezer wiped his eyes. "Well, my dear, it's the risk we must all take until an elixir has been created that can reveal a person's very soul." He pinched his white, waxed moustache and stared into the trees. "I could make a lot of money with a product like that."

"Can you sing, Miss North?" Miss Miranda stood behind them, her arms folded against her chest. Her lips were set in a tight line, and she looked older in the daylight than she had by the fire last evening.

"Yes, ma'am." A memory flashed into Darla's mind. Spud Jones, the owner of the first saloon she'd been hired at, chewing the ever-present cigar in his mouth and pacing back and forth in front of her. "You sing, girl?" That had been the first question out of a mouth filled with rotten teeth and lips that had managed to steal one kiss before she ran away to the next saloon.

"Never go poking around inside the lead wagon. If you need something ask the Doctor or myself. For today, you will help Johnny with his animals. Miss North, are you listening?"

Darla's head snapped up. "Yes, ma'am. I'll be happy to help in any way I can. I'll go find Johnny right away."

As she went off in search of the young boy, she heard the doctor murmur, "Go easy on her, Miss Miranda. I have a feeling about this one."

People bustled around camp, preparing the wagons for the morning's trip. Darla recognized several of the folks she had met the last evening, including the zanies, who nodded her way.

Johnny lounged on the far side of the animal wagon, wolfing down a chunk of corn bread.

Darla nudged him with her elbow. "Hey, I'm supposed to help you."

"Oh yeah, sure." Johnny leapt to his feet and led the way to the wagon's back end, bits of blond hair waving on his head like tiny flags with each step.

An ornate little door had been built into the side of the cart. Johnny opened this to reveal a small compartment. He reached in and pulled out a pail.

Darla wrinkled her nose.

Johnny grinned. "Pretty rank, ain't it?" He tipped it forward to reveal vegetable peelings and other food scraps inside. "Breakfast for Lucy."

"Who's Lucy?" Darla's mind sifted through the members of the menagerie she had seen last night in the dim light of the lantern.

"She's the pig, of course. Don't you remember?" Johnny set the bucket on the wagon steps. He led Darla through the trees a short way until they came to a large, decaying stump. The boy knelt down under some bushes and drew out three wood and wire contraptions.

"Are those traps?" Darla craned her neck for a better look.

"Yes. They're empty, but that don't matter. Shirley ate last night, and Earl a few days ago. They'll keep."

"Oh. Rats for the snakes?"

"Yep. They're live traps, since the snakes like to catch their dinners." Johnny slipped the traps into a pouch hanging from his belt and headed back to the wagon.

When they passed through the cart's funny little door, they were greeted by a chorus of grunts, chirps and squawks. Two white doves cooed from a second cage Darla hadn't noticed the night before.

"Over there." Johnny pointed to a large jug in the corner. "Could you make sure everyone gets fresh water?"

"Sure." Darla leaned over the pig's pen. Lucy was tiny for a pig, and light pink with gray spots.

The porker swished a small, bare tail and sniffed the air.

"I don't have your food, he does." Darla pointed to Johnny. She grabbed a broom hanging from a nail beside the pen and used it to pull the water dish closer to the bars so it would be easier to reach.

"Don't worry, she won't hurt you." Johnny reached through the bars to scratch Lucy's ears. "She's the nicest pig in the state of Texas."

Lucy closed her eyes and grunted.

"When we stop this afternoon, I'll take her outside for some exercise." Johnny poured his pail of slops into the small trough. "And we'll clean her pen. I swish it out every day. Lucy gets grouchy when her place ain't clean, same as anyone."

Johnny showed Darla how to open the bird cages and slip in their water and food without letting them out.

"Bad girl!" The parrot squawked and snapped at her hand when she reached in for the water dish.

Darla pulled it back quickly. "Goodness, I never had a bird talk to me before!"

"Don't mind Fred." Johnny sprinkled in a handful of food. "He's sassy when he's hungry."

They fed the snowy rabbits and the white mice, which Johnny explained were used in the magic show and not meant for snake food.

The snake cages came last. Darla shuddered as a forked tongue flicked out between the wooden bars.

"I'm not gonna make you touch 'em. Dr. Ebenezer don't let the new girls handle the snakes." Johnny reached in and pulled out a twisting shape. The snake was light tan with dark olive markings along its length. "Come on out, Shirley." The boy placed the creature around his neck, and the snake, after arranging its coils, settled down in apparent contentment.

Johnny handed Darla the water dish, and she hastened to empty, clean and refill it. She placed it back in the cage.

As Johnny finished putting the snake's home to rights, Darla reached out a trembling finger to stroke the reptile's skin. The scales were smooth and cool. The only other time she'd touched a snake was as a child of six, when her dad let her hold the hide of a rattler he'd killed. *It really is beautiful, in a twisty, snaky sort of way.*

After making sure each beast had food and water, Johnny wiped his brow. "Whew, what a job. We should be moving any time now." He counted on his fingers. "Fifteen folks in the troupe now, including the baby. Six or seven of us walk during the day to lighten the load. Everyone takes turns. You have good walking shoes?"

Darla stuck out a foot to reveal her black leather boots. "They aren't pretty, but they'll be fine. I'm going to see if I can help someone else."

"Suit yourself. I'll be out in a minute." Johnny said with a smile. He sat back on his little bench, still holding Shirley. Darla could hear him talking to the snake as she went out of the wagon.

Ketzia moved through the teams of large white horses, checking the harnesses of each team as she went.

"Darla." The gypsy girl's eyes lit up. "Did you sleep all right?"

"Sure. I can sleep anywhere." Darla waved her hand. "But where do you sleep? Are you married?"

"I stay with Fatima and her family. Our people keep separate. It is just our custom," said Ketzia. "I am married, but my love is far away." Her merry face sobered. "Niccolo is with a ranch in Fort Worth. He's earning money so we can save for a house and land of our own."

"I thought gypsies never settled down." Darla surveyed the rows of wagons. The two gypsy wagons were easy to tell from the others, with their rounded tops and brightly colored exteriors.

"He and I have traveled with family all our lives." Ketzia leaned against the creamy white flank of a lead horse and tapped on the front of its leg. The animal obediently lifted a massive, feathered hoof, as big as Ketzia's head. She picked at the dirt with a sharp stick. "First when we were babies, in Russia."

"You're fine then," Ketzia said to the horse, and lowered the foot back to the ground. "Fifteen years ago, our families sailed on a great ship to America. But now, after our wagon wheels have dug into every road across this land, Niccolo and I are ready for a peaceful home."

"I'm sorry for making assumptions," Darla said. "I've dealt with my own share from other folks."

The gypsy woman laughed. "It's all right. Yours aren't cruel and don't come with thrown rocks."

A shout came from the lead wagon, and it jerked forward. The other carts began to roll after it.

Ketzia leapt to the driver's seat, her long hair billowing behind her like a dark sail. "Ride with me a ways?"

"I'd be delighted." Darla's body was still weary from lack of sleep, and Ketzia seemed like the sort of person she would like to have as a friend. She swung up and into the seat beside her.

"Don't you miss your husband?" she asked Ketzia.

"Very much. He is so kind and very handsome." Ketzia pressed her free hand against her heart. "But he works hard for us, and will come when he can. I send him telegrams so he knows where we are going. And if I am lucky, his letters sometimes reach me too."

Ketzia raised a dark eyebrow at Darla. "And you? There is someone you left behind as well?"

Darla stared out across the fields, green with fresh spring growth. "How did you know?" she finally asked. "Are you one of those fortune-telling gypsies?"

"No, I'm not," Ketzia said in a sharp tone. Her face softened. "I'm sure that's something else you have heard in stories of my people. That we are all pagans and witches?"

Darla nodded, too embarrassed to speak.

"Don't feel bad. Most people think this." Ketzia patted her hand. "No, my family are Christians. Very strong in our faith, as are many Romanis. We only eat certain foods. We have many traditions. It is our way."

"Is that why you don't stay in Miss Miranda's tent?"

"Yes. But . . ." A bright smile spread across Ketzia's face. "I do enjoy making new friends."

Warmth filled Darla's heart despite the chilly spring morning.

"Now, about your young man," Ketzia pressed. "It's not that hard to see, you know. One pining heart recognizes another."

"Oh, I can't say he's *my* young man," Darla brushed her fingertips to a burning cheek. "He probably never wants to see me again."

"But he holds your heart, doesn't he?" Ketzia smiled. "And you hold his. I can almost see it there, beating in the palm of your hand."

Darla glanced down, in spite of herself. "Yes, I suppose we both have . . . well . . . a fondness for each other."

"His parents do not approve?"

"Honestly, I don't think Ma Downs would have minded, except . . ." Darla rested her chin on her hands. "I wasn't who I pretended to be."

"What?" Ketzia leaned back. "You're not Darla?"

"No." Darla had to chuckle. "The name is right. I suppose the way to put it is . . . I'm more than I said I was." She turned her head, and even though no one could possibly hear them above the rattle of the wagon, spoke quietly. "I was a saloon girl."

Understanding dawned over Ketzia's dark, lovely face. "Ah. Served drinks. To men."

"And danced. And sang. I didn't sell myself though. Not once."

Ketzia stared over the broad backs of the horses to the road. "I see."

Darla fought the urge to clutch at the girl's arm. "I've changed so much! I left that place behind forever, five months ago. God provided a way for me to escape. My friend, Soonie, she told me God would forgive me no matter what I'd done, and He did. I prayed with Brother Jenkins and accepted Jesus in my heart."

Ketzia twisted the reins tighter around her hands. "Then why did you not explain these things to your man? He deserves to know. Does this man love God?"

Darla bowed her head. "Yes, he does. Very much. That's what made it so hard, Ketzia."

"If he follows God, then he knows about forgiveness. And he might be able to forgive your past, if he truly loves you."

Darla's eyes filled with tears. "But how could he forgive the lying? Don't you see now why I had to leave?"

Ketzia bit her lip and nodded. She stared down at the reins in her hands. "I still think he might forgive you, though. If you only tried."

She doesn't even know me, and yet she cares so much. "I don't know. I think it's too late."

They rode in silence for a long time, listening to the hooves clopping and the jingle of the harnesses.

ANGELA CASTILLO

14

Ethan's Choice

"They took the northeast road, and that's all I know." The bearded man scratched his jaw. "These medicine show folks don't say much. I'm not liable to ask questions unless I have a suspicion."

"I see." Ethan tried to remain calm, but his fingers twitched on Jack's reins. *Darla's already so far away.* "You're certain the girl was with them? And she didn't seem to be in trouble?"

"Depends on what you call trouble. She wasn't hurt or nothing, if that's what you mean. Said she was their sister, or some such." The man tipped back his hat and raised a bushy eyebrow. "Never could get the gist of what she was telling me. She's crazy as a bat, that one. You the fellow she was gonna run away with?"

Ethan shrugged. "I don't know anything about that. I'm her friend and I'm worried about her. That's all."

The bearded man sighed. "Well, that's good, what with her father's health." He gave Ethan one last searching look. "If you'll 'scuse me, I ain't had my breakfast." He turned and ambled off in the direction of the food stands.

Drops of sweat beaded Ethan's forehead. *Darla told us her parents had been dead for years.* He shrugged. The guard didn't seem to be the brightest individual. Whatever happened, the man must have misunderstood the situation.

The horse pawed the ground. Ethan clicked his tongue and tapped his heels into the heaving flanks. "Come on. Let's see if you can catch up with them." *The northeast road heads out of the city. I'll see if that guard was right about that much at least.*

Ethan patted his saddlebags. He'd come to the fair on a hunch, and had hoped to goodness Darla might still be there. *At least I have enough food to last a few days.*

Before leaving Downs House, he'd darted into the kitchen for provisions, where he'd had a confrontation with Mrs. Betty.

"Your heart's gonna break in two again if you get mixed up with that girl. You should just let her go, that's what I think," she had warned. "And what will your ma say?"

"I'm a grown man, Mrs. Betty. I told Ma where I'm going, and she understands. The house will be fine without me, and I'll only be gone a few days at the most. I have to go. If I don't . . . I have to at least try this time."

Creases had formed on the dark forehead and she'd pursed her lips. "Go with Jesus, boy. And may He hold your heart together even though you insist on tossing it out in the dirt." She'd waved him away and turned back to her stove.

I have money. A lump formed in his throat. He'd gone into town first, to see if anyone had seen Darla. He'd wondered around for an hour before he'd remembered her mentioning the medicine show and how much fun it might be to join one.

He'd hesitated only a moment before walking into the store. Ethan knew the fiddle wasn't worth the crisp bills the man had placed in his hand.

"I'll keep it for you awhile," the shopkeeper had promised. "You can buy it back."

Ethan shook his head. *If I can't find Darla, I'm not sure if I'll want to play again, anyway.*

After a half hour of riding, something else the fairground guard had said floated up in Ethan's mind, and he drew up the reins. The horse tossed its head and played with the bit. "Sorry, Jack." *Feller she was running away with.* The words tickled his conscience, like those gnats that came out in flurries at the end of summer.

The red-haired man last night. Darla knew his name. Could he have been a former lover? *But why would she pretend to care for me when she loved someone else?* Did she care? She had flirted with him, but that could have just been her playful nature shining through.

Would Darla run away with another man without even saying goodbye? He clenched his fist and held it to his forehead, forcing the air to come in slow, even breaths. *I will not give in to the anger.*

Jack shifted from foot to foot, waiting. Ethan stared down the road, counting the birds that swooped down to pick up worms from the mud.

Finally, Ethan clicked his tongue and urged the horse forward. *This time, I have to know.*

###

Doctor Ebenezer used a leathered finger to trace the mysterious symbols carved into the tree trunk. "Yep, looks about right. Kickapoo Medicine Company came through, but it says April 1899. Two years is plenty of time."

"All the shows leave notes for each other on message trees," Johnny whispered to Darla. "That way, folks have time to save up money again before another troupe comes by."

"And to forget any stomach cramps or septic fits the last batch of remedies gave them," Ketzia added, rolling her eyes.

Darla had settled into the travel lifestyle fairly well in the two days since she'd joined the caravan. Her shoes were the only things she'd taken from the items Downs House had provided for her. She'd left one of her precious half-dollars to pay for them, along with the note of explanation.

The note hadn't really explained much of anything. She'd thanked them, of course, and included as much of an apology as would fit on the bit of paper, a link of the chain she had saved from the orphan's Christmas party.

She sighed and moved over to the barrel set up on a wooden crate beside the lead wagon. A community cup hung from a nail on the side and she filled it with water and took a small sip. Better not to think about Down's House. Thoughts like that would lead to Ethan and . . . *Oh.* The cup slid from her fingers and clattered to the ground.

Peter, one of the two youngest gypsy boys, ran over and handed it back to her. "Here you go, Miss Darla." His smile was so sweet and full of innocence; she couldn't help but return it.

Music floated through the camp, and she wandered over to the fire. Ketzia's father, Mr. Shishkeer, and Ketzia's brothers, Fonso and Pasha, played a lively tune. Ketzia twirled to the rhythm, banging her tambourine. The musical notes danced in the afternoon breeze, almost tangible. *Perfect to keep me from thinking about Downs House and . . . him.*

Pasha was married to Fatima, but Fonso winked and twirled his long, thick moustache at Darla whenever she passed by. But he never spoke to her. Darla wasn't used to being treated with such indifference, especially by a dashing young man, but it didn't bother her. Only one man held her heart, and she ached to hear his voice.

Shaking her head, she tried to focus on the upcoming show. She'd already practiced her 'bit,' as Johnny called it, for the performance. The costume and play seemed innocent enough, nothing she would blush for doing, even if Brother Jenkins happened to be in the crowd. Still, the true purpose of the presentation didn't make much sense.

Doctor Ebenezer assured her all would be revealed when the time came. He wanted her to learn as she went. "Keeps you on your toes," he'd added cryptically.

Plenty of mysteries had presented themselves for her to mull over during the hours of travel while she trudged beside the wagons. What did Doctor Ebenezer actually sell? The only medicine she'd seen was the bottle he had 'dosed' her from at the fair gates, but these wagons must hold hundreds of dollars' worth of products to fund so many people and animals. *What is in the lead wagon? Why can't I see it? If I'm going to be part of the show, I should know all about it, shouldn't I?*

Darla had never seen a medicine show in action, though she'd heard tales from a few cowboys who'd been to them.

While Darla gazed at the fire, Fatima came by with bundles in her arms, heading in the direction of a nearby stream.

Must be doing laundry. Darla raised her head. "Ketzia?" she called to her friend.

"Yes?" The girl put down her tambourine and came over, silk skirts swirling around her feet.

"Isn't the performance tonight? I thought the town was less than a mile away."

"No, no." Ketzia shook her head. "The zanies will be the only ones in town tonight. They'll talk to the city leaders to make sure our show is welcome. It's their job to find a good location for us to hold the show, and they post hand-bills so everyone will know when to come." She pulled a piece of paper covered with block-printed letters from the pocket of her skirt. "We'll arrive a half-hour after we're supposed to be there. The crowd will be foaming at their mouths, waiting for us."

"Oh." Darla pulled off her hat and fluffed a few of the feathers that looked a bit droopy. "I suppose that makes sense."

Mrs. Miranda had been cooking something in her giant pot, and Johnny, Doctor Ebenezer, and a few other members of the troupe were already lined up with bowls in their hands. Darla rose to get her share, but turned back to Ketzia. "Why doesn't your family eat with the rest of us?"

Ketzia folded her arms. "You eat white folk's food. Just like our people only marry within our group, we also have rules about food and how it is prepared. It's part of our faith."

"I see." Darla had woken every morning to pray and read a few words from her worn Bible. *Should I be doing more?* "Where do you go to church?"

Ketzia lowered her eyes. "Doctor Ebenezer has a little prayer service for the troupe on Sundays. Our people are not allowed in town churches. Even if we were . . . church for us is different. We left all the gypsy churches behind, in

Russia. Now our church is inside here." She tapped her heart.

A lump rose in Darla's throat as she remembered Sundays from a not-so-distant past. Churchgoers would stream from the building, giving her scandalized glances. Not that she blamed them. She'd thought nothing of standing outside in petticoats with crimson garters and skirts cut above her knees. Though some of the men who'd given her the most aggrieved stares from beside their wives on Sunday mornings had whistled the loudest when she danced on Monday nights.

"Are you thinking about your man?" Ketzia gave her a sympathetic smile.

Darla glanced around, realizing she was standing stock-still in between the fire and the food line. She hastily grabbed a bowl, allowed Miss Miranda to fill it, and went back to sit beside her friend.

"No, I wasn't thinking about Ethan. My old life . . . I don't want to go back to that place ever again, even in my mind."

"The doctor always says the past stays with us so we won't trip up in our future," said Ketzia. "He's wise, for a white man."

"The troupe seems to trust him."

Ketzia pulled off a gold bracelet and spun it around her finger. "Yes, we do. He has kept food in our bellies and money in our pockets, and treated us more fairly then any other mountebank we have worked for. I suppose you could say he has proven himself."

Darla shivered as a breeze sifted through the thin material of her dress. Though thankful for the quick friendship that had sprung up between herself and Ketzia, she wondered if she could truly trust the doctor.

15

Brambles

*F*og hung in clouds over the fields, but even the thickest patches couldn't hide the bright green hills. Spring was coming. Ethan always thought of the season as a tall woman with clothing woven from willow branches, strewing wildflowers through the woods with graceful sweeps of her arm. *She has flowers in her golden curls, and dimples that flash when she smiles.*

Ethan shook his head. *Darla again.* He couldn't push her from his thoughts, not even for a moment.

Trees parted to the left, and he rode into a clearing. *Someone camped here recently, maybe even last night.*

He dismounted and hunched over, examining the ground. Giant marks rutted the ground, most certainly created by large, heavy wagons. The ground in one area was churned and furrowed from the hooves of at least a dozen draft horses.

The fire pit in the middle of camp was still smoking. Only a few inches down, he found warm embers. After coaxing the flames back to life, he toasted his own bread on them. A strange comfort filled him. *Perhaps Darla warmed herself by this very fire.*

"We ought to hurry," he told Jack, who was pulling up tender shoots of grass at the clearing's edge. "There's no reason we can't catch up with them by tonight."

A nagging voice wormed its way into his mind. *And if she doesn't want you to find her? What then?*

Ethan tidied up from lunch, raked dirt back over the fire, and climbed on Jack.

The fog gradually burned away, leaving fields brimming with violet Spiderworts, pink primroses, and in some places, acres of bluebonnets stretching out like waves of the ocean.

"No other land could have flowers prettier than Texas," Ethan murmured.

Brush grew thicker on the sides of the road. Oak and elm trees pressed in, boughs embracing to create a leafy tunnel over the lane.

Ethan stopped to take a drink from his canteen. "We've made pretty good time, Jack. Shouldn't be much longer." He placed the container back in his pack.

Loud crackles sounded from the bushes, growing closer. *Must be a deer.*

A horse crashed though the trees in front of them and bolted across the path. Jack tossed his head and danced to the side.

"Easy, easy," Ethan held the reins with one hand and patted Jack with the other. "Calm down."

The other horse lumbered off through the underbrush and disappeared.

Ethan spoke soothing words to his horse while he considered the situation. The animal hadn't been a draft horse, like the ones pulling the caravan. It was a sturdy riding mount with a plain saddle and bridle, the kind any local farmer could have owned.

Ethan peered down the path of broken bracken the horse had left in its wake. "Jack, I think we need to see what's going on over here."

Deep hoof prints in the soft earth made backtracking easy. Ethan ducked down to avoid low-hanging branches. The horse hadn't bothered to follow any man-made path in its mad dash through the trees.

A low moan came through the woods.

Jack snorted and jerked his head, the whites of his eyes showing.

"Smell something you don't like?" Ethan pulled his shotgun from its saddle holster and slid down from the broad back.

Only a small ways in and he stopped short. A man's boot protruded from a clump of bushes.

Ethan stepped closer and nudged it with his toe.

Another moan sounded from inside the brush.

Pushing into the sticks, Ethan found the owner of the foot, tangled in the brambles. He put his gun back into the holster on Jack's back and pulled out his Bowie knife. Hacking away at the brush, he freed the man, one branch at a time.

"Sir, are you all right?"

The only answer was a low sigh.

His efforts finally allowed him to clear the man's face, which was pale and sagging with wrinkles. His hair would have been colored salt-and-pepper if a large wound on his forehead hadn't darkened it to a sticky scarlet.

"We'd better get you out of here." Ethan untangled the remaining thorns from the man's upper torso. He drew a clean handkerchief from his pocket and shook his head. *Not big enough.* Returning to Jack, he pulled his only shirt from his pack. As he tore it into strips, his finger brushed against a row of coarse stitches where a hole had been mended in the sleeve.

Darla did that. He knew it was her work because she was the woman least handy with a needle in Downs house and she'd apologized for the quality of mending when she'd returned it. He didn't care about the haphazard stitching; he liked having something she'd touched so close to himself.

No one can fix the shirt now. Would a similar fate be in store for the feelings that had grown in his heart over the last few months?

Ethan folded the cloth and pressed it against the wound. After a short time, the flow of blood turned to a trickle. He wrapped another strip of his shirt around the man's head to hold the makeshift bandage in place.

Rocking back on his heels, he watched the cloth. Blood seeped through to make a dime-sized splotch, but grew no bigger.

The man's eyes fluttered open. "Hey," he said in a weak voice. Moving his head, he winced.

"Yeah, best not to do that yet." Ethan rolled up what was left of his shirt and placed it beneath the man's head. "I'm Ethan Downs."

"Frank Duncan." The man moved his hand as if to offer to shake, and then clutched at his side. "Ouch! That blasted horse! Rabbit ran right under his hooves and spooked the daylights out of him. Don't know how long I've been laying here."

Ethan glanced over at the blood stain on the dirt beneath the brambles. "Not for long. Or you might not be alive to talk about it." At fifteen, Ethan had worked for a farmer. One of the man's hired hands had been pinned by a thresher. The man had been alone in the field, and had bled to death before Ethan had found him.

The blood pooled on the forest floor here was almost as abundant. *Good thing I don't have a weak stomach.* "If I hadn't seen your horse thundering down the path, I would have kept going." He held his canteen to the man's lips.

Mr. Duncan guzzled the water. After he had his fill, he pushed himself up on an elbow, but quickly sank back down. "Oh, I'm seeing the little stars shining bright, that's for sure."

"You lost some blood there." Ethan craned his neck to look into the trees. Not another soul in sight.

"I was by myself, on my way to town," the elderly man explained. "But my house ain't far from here. Jerusha's my wife. She knows a bit about doctoring. She'll help me if I can just get to her."

"All right." Every moment Darla was riding further away, and the road ahead held dozens of twists and turns. *Surely the show'll set up shop in the nearest town. Jack's fast. I'll make it.* He couldn't very well leave Mr. Duncan in the woods by himself.

Ethan examined the cloth around the man's head. The blood stain hadn't grown any larger. He pressed his lips together and nodded. "This is going to be tough, but if your house is as close as you say, it would be better to get you there and find some help."

Mr. Duncan closed his eyes. "Sounds best."

Ethan grabbed Mr. Duncan's arm and hooked it over his own shoulders. He pulled the man to a sitting position. Mr. Duncan howled and pressed a hand to his side again.

Pulling the homespun shirt up, Ethan found a reddened patch of skin.

"Yep, you banged it up pretty good. You'll have a real nice bruise there by tomorrow, Mr. Duncan."

The man gritted his teeth as Ethan prodded the area with gentle fingers. "Musta landed on a rock," he grunted.

"You might have cracked a rib, but I don't think so. Of course, I'm not a doctor." He hoisted Mr. Duncan up once more. "Are we ready, then?"

Mr. Duncan grimaced. "I'm not sure. I feel like Old Nick's dancing on my innards. I'll do my best."

With a bit of effort and more than a few choice words from the old man, Ethan finally got him up on Jack's back. He led his horse down the path indicated by Mr. Duncan, stopping every few steps to make sure he was secure in the saddle.

The old man's face changed to various shades of red, and he moaned when Jack stepped a bit too heavy on the rough dirt path. Ethan could tell he worked hard to hide the bulk of the pain he must be enduring. He'd shift his right or left hand when they'd come to a fork in the path. Ethan would trudge onward after cutting a section of bark from a nearby tree to make sure he could find his way out.

Finally, the scent of smoke tinged the air, and clucks of chickens reached Ethan's ears. A small brown house appeared in a clearing. A wizened old woman bent over a garden, pulling weeds in a methodical fashion. Her hair was smoothed back into a little white knot at the nape of her neck. Though made of simple cloth, her clothes were tidy and well mended.

The old woman's head snapped up as the small party crashed through the trees. Her gaze landed on the crumpled man in Jack's saddle, and she leapt to her feet. "Oh Frankie, what happened to you? Oh my lord, was it bandits? Are you a bandit?" This question was directed towards Ethan. She reached over and grabbed a hoe, a dangerous glint in her faded blue eyes.

"No, no," Mr. Duncan said, chuckling a bit as Ethan lowered him from the saddle. "It's that blasted horse. Got spooked. I suppose I lost him. And good riddance."

As if in reply, the runaway horse trotted around the side of the chicken coop, dipped his head, and pulled a mouthful of clover from the ground. He looked up at the cluster of humans, chewed a moment, and then swallowed.

"I've never seen a horse look so smug," said Ethan.

"Told you not to try to ride that animal, Frankie Duncan." Mrs. Duncan walked over and scooped up the animal's trailing reins. "Best let this nice man help you inside so I can check you over."

She jerked at the horse's halter. "And *you* better consider yourself lucky I don't shoot you and sell you for dog meat."

Ethan helped Mr. Duncan through the small door. The one room house had a cast-iron stove in one corner and a bed in another. A wooden chest, two chairs and a table completed the furniture collection.

"Take him over to the bed. Hopefully he won't bleed out on the way there." Mrs. Duncan's tone was irritated, but her eyes were full of concern.

Ethan stooped to keep from hitting his head on the low roof. He climbed up the old-fashioned step-stool and hoisted Mr. Duncan on to the four-poster bed.

Mr. Duncan rolled over and lay flat out on the bed. "Oh, I am glad to be here and not out in that thorn bush! Lordy, I thought I was a goner!"

"You're too cantankerous to keel over that easy." Mrs. Duncan pulled off her husband's boots and covered him with the worn blanket. She poured water from the stove into a dish and brought it to the bed, along with some clean cloths.

"I'm going to take a look. Good patch-up job, by the way," she said to Ethan as she examined the bandage.

"Thank you. It started out as a nice shirt, too."

When she pulled back the cloth, a hand crept to her cheek. "Land sakes, Frankie!"

She turned and studied Ethan. An old clock on the mantle ticked away several seconds before she spoke, this time in a softer tone. "I thank you for saving my Frank's life."

"Oh, anyone would have done it." Ethan shrugged. "It was just me that happened by."

"God sent you, and that's the truth." She patted at the wound with her cloth. The gash was about two inches long beneath the blood, and gaped open wide enough to fit a penny inside, lengthwise. The lump beneath it had already turned a purplish-green.

"Ah, Frankie, you could never do things halfway." Though an admonishment, the words were delivered in a sweet, soothing tone. "I'll have to stitch it closed-- we don't want that handsome forehead all marked up. But I've done it before, haven't I?" She traced another scar on Mr. Duncan's temple with a leathered finger.

Ethan rocked back on his heels. His heart urged him to jump on Jack and gallop off to Darla, now that his passenger had been delivered.

Mrs. Duncan's hands shook while she attempted to thread a needle. She held it out to Ethan. "Would you mind? It's hard for me now, in this light."

I can't leave. Not yet. Ethan took the needle. "I'll stay and help you get the stitching done."

"Thank you, son. Won't take me long."

Flickering candles had replaced the daylight by the time the little procedure was completed.

Mrs. Duncan served Ethan a steaming bowl of stew that had been simmering on the stove. "Might as well stay the night. Won't do to bluster into those woods with the dark upon you. We have a loft upstairs, where my boy sleeps. He's out of town for a few days, so you're free to use it."

Ethan nodded glumly. He could only hope the medicine show would linger in town a bit longer.

Mrs. Duncan settled into a rocker that must have been made when time began, cupping her own bowl of soup in careful hands. "So, what brings you to our neck of the woods?"

"A woman." Ethan saw no reason to hide the truth, and found surprising comfort in speaking the words aloud.

"I see." She sipped her stew and then contemplated her empty spoon in the firelight. "You from Dallas, then?"

"Yes."

"That's a big place." She gave him a slanted look. "Lots of ladies to choose from. What makes this girl so special? She must be awful pretty."

Darla's smile flashed into Ethan's mind like a shooting star. "She is beautiful, but, ah, there's something more. When she walks into a room, everything changes." He rubbed his chin. "The colors get brighter."

A slow smile spread across Mrs. Duncan's wrinkled face. "Hmmm. She sounds pretty wonderful."

"It's not only all that. She has such a caring heart. Tries to find the worth in people, show them they have something great inside of them. So many girls worry about how their hair looks, or keeping up with the latest clothing styles. That's not Darla. She wants to help everyone."

Mrs. Duncan patted his hand. "Sounds like the two of you make the perfect pair."

16

First Act

"Hup!" One of the zanies--Darla never could be quite sure whether it was Simon or Aaron though both flirted with her shamelessly-- tossed flaming batons into the air.

"Hup, hup." The other zany caught them and tossed them back. The movements were fluid as walking, breathing. A part of every day life.

Hands and flames moved faster and faster. The crowd held a collected breath of wonder.

"Hup!" The clowns somersaulted forward, landing with even thumps on the rough wooden boards of the stage, each catching two still-lit batons.

Darla applauded along with the audience. Though the flames burned brighter when the brothers practiced at night, the energy and awe of the crowd made the act even more exciting. Behind the stage, an expansive field of newly-planted corn flowed as far as the eye could see.

The next segment belonged to Miss Miranda. The stately coils of hair, usually piled high on her head, had been transformed into thick braids that hung down over each shoulder, almost to her knees. A deep purple robe was wrapped around her and she wore silver slippers with pointed toes. The transformation was so complete Darla would never have guessed this could be the same genteel woman, except that she'd helped braid the dark hair this morning.

Doctor Ebenezer stepped out ahead of Miss Miranda and bowed to the audience. "Ladies and gentlemen, we will now show you the creatures that provide our most valuable ingredient. A patented formula no man can reproduce . . ."

CLANG! Somewhere off stage, a pair of cymbals banged together.

The doctor held out his hand. "I present to you the Lady Lazerleena, from the mysterious country of Bangladesh!"

Darla knew for a fact Miss Miranda had been born and raised in Oklahoma, but the crowd gave an appreciative 'oooooh' as the woman stepped out.

Miss Miranda swept across the stage, her robe swishing about her ankles. Darla squinted. One of the snakes hung in placid coils around the woman's smooth, white neck, so still he almost looked like a third braid.

Many members of the crowd seemed to spy the snake at the same time; and there were gasps and squeals from the women. Murmuring rose up among the people, and some folks backed away from the stage.

Doctor Ebenezer held out his hands. "Calm down, folks. I can assure you this creature will do you no harm, though he was once deadly as sin itself. After being tamed by the most skilled snake charmer in Bora-Bora, he's as gentle as any kitten. Observe."

Miss Miranda walked around the stage, stroking the snake's coils and humming a little tune as she moved. The snake slipped down her arm and coiled around her wrist like a thick, live bracelet. The woman seemed mesmerized by the reptile's movement. In a sudden, swift motion, she planted a kiss on its head.

The crowd gasped and burst into applause.

Miss Miranda gave a demure smile and bowed, the snake still gracing one arm. She stepped off the stage and walked through the crowd, which parted like the Red Sea before her. A row of buildings stood behind the audience and she disappeared behind them.

I'm glad they didn't ask me to hold a snake. Darla's heart beat faster at the thought.

Doctor Ebenezer waited for the applause to die away. "Yes, folks, we obtain the finest snake oils from our friend there. The snake, tame as he is, is pleased to contribute to the health and happiness of all upon this earth."

He held up a yellow bottle, so tiny Darla could barely make out the shape.

"This bottle may not look like much, but the ointment inside can cure arthritis, vertigo, impetigo, heartworm, ringworm, and even the common cold."

"Is it really snake oil?" Darla hissed to Johnny Jingles, who stood beside her and waited to go on for their act.

"Nope," Johnny Jingles rolled his eyes. "But it will help to cure lots of ailments. The doctor just dresses up the truth a bit, that's all."

Darla's shoulders sagged. *Should I be a part of something that deceives people, no matter how helpful it may be?* One of the nuns at the orphanage had tried to convince her to take some nasty-smelling medicine once when she'd been sick.

After many failed attempts, the elderly woman had told her it was angel juice from Heaven. The ruse had worked, and she'd gulped it down. Later she'd realized the woman had fibbed because Darla had been dangerously ill and the woman was terrified she'd lose her.

She shook her head. The Bible clearly said not to lie. *Oh God, what should I do?*

Johnny went up on the stage, dressed in his colorful costume and jingling shoes. He used his fingers to give a loud whistle. Lucy, the pig, pranced out in a ruffled collar.

The crowd gave the loudest applause of the night as the tiny pig wove in and out of Johnny's feet, fetched a ball, and jumped through a hoop.

Holding out the hoop for a second time, Johnny whistled the pig's signal.

Lucy hesitated and backed away. She plopped down on her hindquarters, sticking her wrinkled nose up into the air.

"Lucy, jump." Johnny said in a threatening tone. He shook the hoop.

The pig glanced back at him, grunted, and turned her back to the boy.

The crowd howled with laughter. One man shouted, "Bacon for supper, then, kid?"

Johnny's face grew red. Fumbling in his pocket, he drew out a gun. He aimed it at the tiny pig and pulled the trigger.

BANG! A bright flash lit the stage.

Lucy fell to the stage, her little cloven hooves sticking up like pins in a cushion.

The crowd gasped. A baby cried.

The zanies rushed in with a tiny stretcher. One brother examined the stiff little body and shook his head. "Nothing we can do." They rushed out again, leaving the pig behind.

Darla took a deep breath. *My turn.*

She moved to the stage with tentative steps. Her nerves bunched up in her stomach like writhing vines. *I've performed a hundred times for a much rowdier crowd. I can do this.*

She moved out on the rough boards and stretched an arm out to Johnny Jingles. "What have you done? This animal was my only companion. My dearest friend!"

Johnny covered his face with his hands and ran off the stage.

"My poor darling." Darla held out her hands to the motionless pig. "You are gone from this world, but not from my heart." She dabbed her eyes with a handkerchief, turned to the crowd, and began to sing.

"In the sweet
by and by,
We will rest on that beautiful shore."

Darla warbled as pitifully as she could. The pig stayed motionless at her feet for the entire song.

Most of the women and a few of the men were wiping their eyes and clearing their throats by the final verse.

After the last melancholy note, Doctor Ebenezer ran back on stage, his coat tails flapping. "My dear lady, what seems to be the trouble?"

Darla gestured to Lucy. "Oh, Doctor, it's my little Flossy. She has passed on to the great unknown before her time. My only comfort in this cruel, hard world has left me!" She buried her face in her black mantilla.

"Never fear!" Doctor Ebenezer pulled a small canister from his never-ending supply of coat pockets. He held it out to the crowd. "An old Indian medicine man gave me the secret ingredients for this potion. One of these pills will pull any creature from the very jaws of death."

Darla felt the hot breath of the crowd on her skin as they drew closer to watch.

The doctor shook a small white pill into his hand, opened Lucy's mouth, and pushed it in.

The pig trembled, and her legs twitched. With a little squeal, she jumped to her feet and darted down the stage. She disappeared over the side, where Johnny was hidden and waiting for her.

Applause thundered once more. Darla bowed and left the stage, stepping lightly now that her performance was over.

Doctor Ebenezer's voice prattled on behind her, expounding on the virtues of his elixirs and pills.

Johnny stood to the side, a grin covering his freckled face. "You did a tip-top job," he said. "I've never seen a crowd cry so much."

"I'm kind of surprised. Aren't these all farmer's families?" Darla asked. "Some probably had bacon for supper!"

"Silly, they didn't cry for the pig." Johnny's eyes shone. "They cried because your voice is so purty."

Fatima came over and handed Darla the baby, her scarlet scarves swishing as she walked. Darla cuddled the bright-eyed child as his mother and big brothers danced on the stage with flaming hoops and torches. Soon the show ended. Crowds lined up all the way around the stage, coins clinking in their hands.

Miss Miranda tugged on Darla's elbow. "This way, Miss North. Doctor Ebenezer doesn't like troupe members to watch the exchange of money . . . makes him nervous."

"Well, all right." Darla headed back to the wagons.

Why would Doctor Ebenezer care about that? Ketzia had told her what the troupe members got paid and it seemed more than fair. In fact, the sum was twice what she made at the nicest saloon she'd worked at. Darla was thrilled with the prospective amount she could make. Money earned would be money saved. With food and a place to sleep already provided, she shouldn't have too many expenses. After saving enough, she'd travel to a respectable city, perhaps even in a different state. Maybe she'd get a good job, like she'd planned after deciding to run off with Soonie and the Comanche people.

Miss Miranda always twists the truth, just a little, and I can never see why. Darla shrugged. In her former profession, she'd come across people who couldn't seem to tell the truth. Sometimes it was out of habit, sometimes as a defense. Maybe the snake charmer was the same way.

As she neared the wagons, a lullaby rose above the trees. Fatima sat by the fire once more, singing to her baby and her boys. Darla had come to look forward to this time at day's end. She had no memory of anyone singing her to sleep, though she liked to think her mother might have done so before she passed on.

Out of sight among the bushes, Darla watched Fatima's eyes glisten as she looked down at her little ones.

I want that. Darla stood still for a moment and pressed her hand against her chest. *I want babies to sing for, someday.*

The animal wagon sat deserted, but any moment Johnny and Miss Miranda would be back to check on things. Darla sat on the small outside stoop. She swung her feet like a girl.

Feeling around in her pocket, she drew out the wooden rose Ethan had given her at Christmas. She always kept it with her, finding its warmth to be her only comfort at times.

The folks in the medicine show were fascinating, and most of them seemed kind enough, but that commandment, "Thou shalt not lie," kept going through

Darla's mind. What would Ma Downs and Ethan think of the show?

Does Ethan miss me? This thought struck her so suddenly she flinched. Tears trickled down her cheeks and she wiped them away with a black taffeta sleeve.

"Thinking about your man?" Ketzia stood beside her, a sympathetic smile on her face.

Darla nodded. "I try not to, but sometimes I can't help it."

Ketzia held out her hand. "Perhaps these will make you feel better." She dropped three small red candies on Darla's lap.

Darla gasped. "Gumdrops? Where did you get them?" She put the rose back in her pocket.

"I bought them at the general store. Sometimes I just need a sweet or two."

Ketzia scooted up next to her, and the two women swung their feet and ate candy until the rest of the troupe came back.

17

Explanations

Ethan was wakened by a thin string of sunlight that stung his eyes the morning after he found Mr. Duncan in the woods. He sat up on the thin straw tic and promptly sneezed. Though Jerusha Duncan kept a clean house down below, she probably left the upstairs housekeeping to her son, and it seemed to Ethan that her fussy nature had not been passed down to him.

After dressing hastily, Ethan climbed down the rough wooden ladder to the tiny room below. Mrs. Duncan was in the same place he'd left her last night, bathing her husband's forehead.

"Good morning. He's caught a slight fever." The old woman pursed her lips. "It's to be expected. I'm not seeing much redness around the wound, so I'll dose him with a fever draught. He'll be all right."

Ethan walked over and stared down at the old man, curled up on the bed in his long john underwear. *His breathing looks even.* "Did he have any fits?"

Mr. Duncan opened one eye and glared at them. "It's not like I can't hear you. Fellow's got ears."

I have to go today. I can't wait any longer. Ethan stepped outside to check Jack. Horses neighed for their breakfast and the cows bellowed pitifully, their swollen udders almost dragging the ground. *I can't leave the Duncans in this state.*

Relief flooded Mrs. Duncan's face when he told her this news. "Don't worry," she assured him. "My son should be back by this evening. If you could stay until then, he can help us out."

Three days later, Ethan leaned against a hoe and surveyed the potato field. Digging out the rocks hadn't been a difficult job. The Duncans had been in the area for years and there weren't many left. But he'd had to find a distraction from the ticking clock.

Mr. Duncan's fever had broken yesterday, and he'd sat up for some breakfast this morning.

Branches crackled from across the field, and Ethan turned to see a young man riding through the front yard. Chickens skittered across the dirt to avoid the thudding hooves.

The man heaved his bulk from the saddle and tied the reins to a tree. When he removed his ten-gallon hat, Ethan could see a strong resemblance to Mr. Duncan.

Mrs. Duncan came outside, wiping her hands on her apron. When she caught sight of the young man, she dropped the cloth, ran to him, and threw her arms around his neck. "Richard, where have you been?"

The young man stepped back and mopped his face with a handkerchief. "Sorry, mother, didn't mean to worry you. The boss added a few days work to the job." He held a hand out to Ethan. "Not sure who you are, mister, but howdy."

Ethan shook the giant hand, a sigh of relief escaping his lips.

"Richard, meet Ethan Downs," Mrs. Duncan said. "This young man saved your father's life." She turned to Ethan, a smile cracking over her thin mouth. "Now you can be on your way to find your lady friend."

Ethan squinted at the sun, sunk low in the horizon. All these days he'd been here, with no choice but to watch the great ball rise and plummet, his heart falling with it every night. He looked back at Mrs. Duncan and tried to return her smile. "Yep, I'll pack up my things."

Mrs. Duncan took his earth-covered hand and pressed it to her cheek. "Dear man. Don't worry; God will lead you to her, if it's meant to be."

###

After a few days on the road, the caravan approached another town. But the doctor shook his head when he studied the mysterious symbols on the message tree. "Been a doings two months past." He gave a handful of coins to one of the zanies. "Aaron, take your brother and get some supplies. Not too much. We don't want folks to know how many of us are out here." His bushy eyebrows drew together. "And no juggling."

"Would you like me to go along?" asked Ketzia. "Fatima and I have scarves and bracelets to sell."

Doctor Ebenezer nodded. "Get a feel for the town, though. If folks don't want you there, don't try too hard."

Relief flooded through Darla. She wasn't quite ready for another performance. Besides, she had to learn a brand-new act, since Doctor Ebenezer didn't like to use the same performances in towns too close together.

Ketzia came out of her family's wagon carrying an armload of bright scarves with intricately beaded patterns.

"Those are lovely," said Darla. "Can you really make money with them?"

"Of course," said Ketzia. "We sell them for a quarter each, some places. Women like to buy them to hang in their windows."

I bet Lisbeth and Patience would both love curtains like that. An unexpected pang of sadness hit Darla. Even though she'd made new friends on her journey with the medicine show, she missed the 'unfortunates' at Downs House. *I wonder if I'll ever see them again.*

A few hours later, when they stopped for the night, Doctor Ebenezer and Johnny taught Darla a new skit. It wasn't much different from the play she'd already learned, but this time it involved her pushing Lucy, complete with a bonnet and nightgown, in a pram and pretending the pig was her child. Lucy was supposed to have come down with some 'ailment' and be on the brink of death.

"Let's try that scene again." Doctor Ebenezer rested his chin on steepled fingers. "I think you could put more emotion into it. After all, it's your own darling child who is sick."

"A rather ugly little tyke." Darla stared into the pram, which was empty for this rehearsal.

She sighed. "Maybe I'm having trouble because I don't know what to believe about your products. Will any of them really help people at all?" A lump rose in her throat. "I should have asked these questions before I did anything, but I got caught up in the rehearsals and learning the skits. I'm sorry."

"I see. Why don't we have a talk?" The doctor gestured for her to sit beside him under the tree.

Johnny glanced at Darla, and then the doctor. "I'm going to check on the snakes. Back in a moment." He walked off towards the wagons.

"I suppose I should start with a bit of my history." Doctor Ebenezer stared off in the distance, a look Darla already recognized as a precursor to a story. "I was married once, very young. My wife and I were both younger than twenty. We found ourselves expecting a child after less than a year of holy matrimony. My parents had provided us with a small home, deep in the back pasture of my father's property, in exchange for my help with farm work. For babies like us, it was a good arrangement. We were the happiest children who ever played house. But then came the morning my wife's birth pains started. . ." He covered his face in his hands.

Darla placed a hand on his arm. "Something went wrong?"

Doctor Ebenezer looked up, his face drawn with pain. "The baby would not come. My mother stayed with my wife, and I galloped off to find the doctor. I found him, and we returned as quickly as possible, but she was already slipping away. I only had a few moments to say goodbye. The baby never even drew its first breath." Tears rimmed the old man's eyes, and he pulled off his spectacles to clean them. "*Her* first breath. Her name was Marian.

"For months, I lived alone in our little house. My mother brought me food that I hardly touched. I became a living skeleton, wrapped in a cocoon of grief.

"One night, I had a dream. My wife came back to me, bathed in the light of Heaven. She told me to take my pain and turn it into something useful, something that could help people."

Darla blinked. "I've never heard of a dream like that."

"Neither had I, but it was as real as this log we're sitting on. I knew God allowed my wife to come and give me that message. I sold everything I owned but the clothes I wore, and begged my parents for money to travel to the Medical School of Cincinnati, where I received my certificate of medicine in 1859.

"The war started soon after, and every bleeder, barber and dentist was forced into service. I didn't want to go, but it was that or flee the country, so I slogged through four years of battlefields. I risked my life and my own limbs, and lopped off dozens of others. But I learned methods that saved many of my patients."

"It must have been terrible." Darla sank back in her seat.

"The sight of so much killing makes you jaded after awhile. But somehow the good Lord kept bitterness and hatred from my heart. I squared my shoulders and made it through the job He set before me.

"After the war, I set up a practice in Ohio. But I found it hard to make progress with the townsfolk. People based medicines on superstitions and old wives' tales. Some methods helped, some were harmless, but most treatments made things worse. Folks were set on the idea that new-fangled doctors didn't know what they were doing. Many times, they were right. Even with all I'd learned, I couldn't help a good portion of the people coming through my clinic's doors.

"So I began to study herbs and old-fashioned treatments. I got a little wagon and went from town to town, speaking to conventional doctors and the 'wise women.' I went to Indian reservations and talked to true medicine men. I spoke to newly freed slave matriarchs who'd been responsible for the health of entire plantations.

Everything I learned, I wrote in journals." He smiled. "I have thirty-six journals now, and soon I'll have thirty-seven. I gathered herbs from a dozen states and made poultices and elixirs. And you know what?" He raised his eyebrows at Darla. "Some of them worked!"

"But if the potions you sell are real, then why stretch the truth?"

"Ah, there's the difficulty." Doctor Ebenezer shook his head. "You're forgetting the part of every human soul that craves a great story. Folks still rely on superstition for much of their beliefs. So I give them a good show. Most towns have no form of entertainment, except for what men find at the saloon. Many folks would pay double what we charge for remedies just to hear a pretty girl sing." He grinned.

"Don't you think we're getting their hopes up? I mean, no medicine can bring back someone from the dead," said Darla.

"It depends on how you look at it," Doctor Ebenezer tilted his head to one side. "For instance, I've developed a chest rub for croup that has saved more children than I can count. I rest easier at night knowing mothers have it in their cabinets. I've discovered treatments for arthritis that can bring feeling and movement back into stiff fingers. I have much truth to offer, though I wrap it up in stories and showmanship. I listen carefully to folk's symptoms and give them the best I have. One thing I refuse to do is plant someone in the crowd and pretend to heal them. And while I travel, I am always looking for more truth, more cures, and more ways to help people. Does this help you understand?"

"I guess so." But another question tugged at the back of Darla's mind. *Why can't I see what's inside the lead wagon? If Doctor Ebenezer was really a good man, why would he keep secrets?*

In her saloon days, she'd run into men who promised her the world. But she'd never believed them. She'd seen other friends taken advantage of by crooks and swindlers, and they'd always been so surprised when they'd been left with broken hearts. *Usually I can tell when men are telling falsehoods. But perhaps Doctor Ebenezer is a better liar than I'm used to dealing with.*

"I'm going to go see if Ketzia needs help," she said to Doctor Ebenezer.

His bushy eyebrows drew together, but he nodded and rolled the pram in her direction. "We'll practice again at the next stop."

18

Treetop

DOCTOR EBENEZER AND
HIS WONDROUS ELIXIRS!

Ethan scanned the handbill--the second such paper he'd found. The first one had been nailed to a fence on the outskirts of a town yesterday. This advertisement was tacked to the wall of the community's general store. Again, he'd arrived too late. He groaned and pulled his hat down over his eyes. *At least I'm still on the right path.*

Despite all the setbacks, Ethan had been confident he could still catch up with the medicine show if he rode hard and fast enough. But now he held the price of all the delays in his hand. Wadding up the paper, he threw it in a nearby spittoon.

"You see the show, Mister?" A gap-toothed man in filthy overalls peered up at him.

"No. Just missed it, I guess. Was it good?"

"Lor', you should've seen it." The man smiled. "Snakes, music, a trained pig . . . and that blond lady."

"Blond?" Ethan's ears perked up. "Did she have dimples? And a beautiful smile?"

"Didn't she though?" The man chuckled. "All her clothes were black, but any man in town would've married her on the spot, if they'd had the courage to ask."

So Darla was still with the caravan a day ago. At least I have that. "I'd really like to see the show. Any idea where they were headed?"

The man scratched his beard. "I think I overheard the doctor say they were heading northwest. Closest town that way would be Willoughby."

I've come this far. Ethan shook the man's grimy hand. "Thank you kindly."

Wiping the clouded mirror with a corner of her shawl, Darla bit her lips and pinched her cheeks. Her heart fluttered down to her stomach and back up again, like a trapped butterfly. *Why am I so nervous? I should be used to this by now.*

"Can I come in?" Ketzia called from outside the tent.

Darla pulled open the flap, and her friend stepped in.

"Are you ready yet? I have something to show you." Ketzia said.

"As ready as I'll ever be." Darla glanced back at the mirror and fluffed her hair. She was wearing the hat she'd bought before she'd joined the medicine show. It rested on her golden curls at just the right angle. *I'm glad I'm not wearing that ugly mourning dress for this performance.*

"Hurry up. You look beautiful as always." Ketzia tugged on her arm.

Darla followed Ketzia away from the tent and down the path to the road.

After a short walk, they entered the town.

Unlike the last village, this one didn't have a platform already made, so the troupe had cleared out the supply buckboard, removed the canvas roof, and staked down the wheels. Crowds of people strained against the makeshift rope barricades.

Ketzia reached an ancient oak tree not far from the improvised stage. A low-hanging branch stretched over the crowd.

Wrapping her arms around a limb, Ketzia kicked off her sandals and gripped the trunk's bark with her bare toes. After a short scramble she was up the tree and sitting on the big branch like a princess on her throne.

"Come on," she called to Darla. "You can see everything from up here."

"Won't Doctor Ebenezer need us?" Darla called back.

Ketzia shielded her eyes and looked over at the stage. She shook her head. "Trust me. It will be a long while."

Darla sighed and regarded the tree. Even after working in saloons, this was right up there with one of the most unladylike things she'd done, at least since the last time she'd climbed a tree at ten years of age. Unbuttoning her shoes, she dropped them in the pile with Ketzia's, and then pulled herself up into the branches.

She settled down beside her friend, only slightly mussed. "You're right. This is a perfect view."

"It's nice, up here in the breeze." Ketzia closed her eyes. "Makes me feel young and free."

Doctor Ebenezer stood on the stage below them, surrounded by the biggest crowd Darla had seen yet.

Wordlessly, he held out a coiled rope, a large iron ring, and a rake. He pushed the rope through the ring, and then wound it around the rake. Each movement was done with precise motions and meticulous care. The crowd watched with bated breath.

After he'd finished this task, the doctor walked through the cleared area around the stage, scanning the ground. On occasion, he picked up rocks to study. Some he'd keep; others he'd toss away. With the selected rocks, he created a little circle in the sand, and then stuck the rake, handle down, into the sand. The rope kept the ring secure to the top of the rake. Smiling in apparent satisfaction, he walked away, leaving the rake where he'd planted it.

During the show, Darla kept waiting for the doctor to do something with the rake, but even after Miss Miranda came out with her snakes, he did not return to it. Finally she turned to Ketzia, whose mouth was turned up at the corners.

"Did he forget about the rake?" she asked.

"Not at all." Ketzia giggled. "He's completely finished with it. Sometimes he does things like that just to mystify the crowd. It's really nothing."

"Oh," Darla said. "Well, it worked on me."

After Miss Miranda's act, Ketzia slid down from the tree, quick as a squirrel.

Darla's ascent was much slower, but she managed to reach the ground with only minor bumps and bruises.

The two women scooted through the crowd and ducked under the rope. Ketzia's father and brothers had already begun a wild tune that swirled through the crowd like a live thing.

Ketzia picked up her tambourine, danced onto the stage and began to play along. Fatima's little boys came onstage to perform flips and somersaults.

Darla's task was to encourage people in the crowd to join in the dance. From the front line, she chose a gentleman with tufts of gray hair and one tooth. He pranced beside her, grinning from ear to ear while his friends clapped and whistled.

After the dance, Darla leaned against the buckboard wheel to catch her breath. A thought dawned on her. *This is the most fun I've had in years.*

Doctor Ebenezer ambled up beside her, mopping his bald head with a large silk cloth emblazoned with strange gold-embroidered patterns. "Darla, I want you to wander out among the crowd. Become a part of it. I've never been to this town before. I'd like to get a better notion of the people we are presenting to."

Darla raised an eyebrow. *Why is he asking me to do this? Surely he would trust a more seasoned member of the troupe than me.* But she nodded and went back out past the ropes. She pushed through the throngs of people, all faces turned towards the stage.

One thing she'd learned during her crazy life was how to read folks, especially men. She could generally tell in the time it took a person to say "How do you do?" if they were good-natured or mean, rich or poor, simple-minded or smart. Every saloon owner of every establishment she had worked said the same thing: "Don't ask for more money than someone has in their pocket, or you won't get anything."

She studied the tired faces of housewives, their work-worn fingers holding the hands of underfed children. Men with unshaved chins and patches in their clothes smiled at the zany's antics. Many folks suffered from some kind of ailment, wearing bandages or eye patches, or leaning on canes. Her heart melted. *All these people in need. God, can Doctor Ebenezer really help them?*

After awhile, she circled back and went to the front of the crowd. Johnny Jingles performed a magic trick with the rabbits. The crowd was hushed, hanging on to every word. Darla smiled. Even at such a young age, Johnny knew how to keep the audience in the palm of his hand.

Darla came up behind the doctor.

He turned and smoothed his moustache. "Well?"

"There's not a person out there with more than a quarter in their pocket. Lots of hard-working folks, many sick or hurt. Looks like these people have been through some tough times."

Doctor Ebenezer nodded. "Just my kind of crowd." He glanced back at her, and a broad grin covered his face, making his cheeks red and round as plums. "My goodness, you should see your face! White as a sheet, my girl!" He held out a small bottle. "Try a drop of that, and you'll be right as rain before your act."

Darla took the bottle and turned it over and over in her hands. She waited until the doctor wasn't looking and placed it in her pocket.

After Darla's skit was finished, she snuck back to the tree, checking over her shoulder to make sure no one was watching. *Miss Miranda wouldn't let me watch before, but I have to see what the doctor is really doing.* Climbing proved a bit harder this time, since twilight had fallen and it was harder to see where to grip. She finally made it to the branch and peered through the leaves.

"Come for a miracle, folks." Doctor Ebenezer had already begun his pitch. "Salves and elixirs to cure what ails ya! Nothing for more than a dime! A dime to fix your troubles!"

Part of the crowd lined up on one side of the wagon to make purchases from Fatima, who collected the money in a box. Darla noticed another group crowding around Doctor

Ebenezer. He had a curious looking object that appeared to be a sort of tube with a cup at the end, almost like a long funnel. He'd hold the cup end of the object to a person's chest, and held the tube to his ear as though he was listening to something.

Suddenly, Darla remembered where she'd seen an object like that before. Once, in a saloon, a man had collapsed after a bar fight. A doctor had come in and used a very similar item to listen to the man's heart.

Another man came up to the doctor, clutching his shoulder.

After a brief conversation, Doctor Ebenezer had the man lie down on a mat on the wagon stage. He laid his hands on the man's shoulder and gave it a shove.

Darla heard bones crack from up in her tree and gasped along with the crowd.

Doctor Ebenezer stood and helped the man to his feet.

The man twisted his arm this way and that, a look of wonder passing over his face. "I'm cured! The pain is gone!"

In the next hour, many people came away from the doctor with smiling faces and bottles of medicine.

For a few of the folks, the doctor had shaken his head and sent them away with empty hands. Darla was glad he didn't try to fill everyone with false hope.

Back at the camp, Darla told Ketzia about the doctor's strange request. "Why do you think he asked me to gauge the crowd like that?"

Ketzia pulled her beaded shawl tighter around her shoulders and stared into the fire. "He never gives that job to anyone besides Miss Miranda or my father. He must think you have a gift."

"A gift?" Darla laughed. "I'm just me."

Ketzia shook her head. "No, I can see it too. You have the ability to discern things about people. My father says it comes from God."

Darla drew up her knees and rested her chin on her folded arms. "I don't know if God is very happy with me right now." A tear rolled down her cheek and she brushed it away.

"Why would you say that?" Ketzia asked.

"Look what I've done. I ran away so the people who took me in out of kindness wouldn't find out who I really was. I stole a man's heart I had no right to claim. And now I'm here. And even though I understand Doctor Ebenezer now, I didn't before, and that makes me worse than any other member of the troupe. I should have made sure the medicines were real before I became a part of selling them to trusting folks."

Ketzia gave her a sympathetic smile. "Oh, Darla, we all go through times of doubt. Think of how I felt, letting my husband go off without me. Every day I wonder if I made the right choice. But there was no place for me at that ranch, and it's only for a short time. I have to trust in God."

"But what if I'm not doing what God wants me to do? What if He never wanted me to come here?"

"Then you have to listen for His voice. He loves you, and He speaks to the children He loves. If you find you are wrong, ask for forgiveness. He'll show you the right path."

Darla nodded. *Somehow, I will make this right.*

Later that night, she opened her Bible to Proverbs chapter 3, verses 5 and 6.

"Trust in the Lord with all thine heart; and lean not unto thine own understanding.

In all thy ways acknowledge him, and he shall direct thy paths."

She lay in the dark a long time, her lips moving in silent prayer so as not to wake the snoring Miss Miranda. "Lord, please help me to trust You. And please direct my path."

19

Suspicion

"We're changing direction." Doctor Ebenezer announced the next morning. The troupe was gathered around the campfire, each absorbed in the little tasks that made up life in the medicine show.

Darla shrugged and went back to darning socks. She didn't care where they went as long as they stayed away from Dallas. Johnny Jingles had assured her they wouldn't visit the same town for at least a year.

"We'll be heading to Waco," Doctor Ebenezer continued. "It's a mighty big city, and they just completed a bridge to span the river a few years ago. There's another town on the way, so we'll see about doing a show there first."

"Waco?" Miss Miranda waved an ostrich plume fan she was repairing. "Those people are so uppity. They'll be even more high and mighty with their fancy new bridge."

"Then we must be even more uppity." Doctor Ebenezer spread out his arms. "Polish the harnesses, bring out the bells. We will out-fancy any fancy they have!" He smiled at Darla. "Especially since we have the fanciest girl of them all, right in our troupe!"

A dark shadow fell over Miss Miranda's face. She dropped her fan and stalked away.

The next day was spent in flurries of preparation. Sequins and feathers were sewn to gowns and hats. New skits were practiced, and Ketzia curled and pinned Darla's hair in dozens of ways to see what suited her best.

"This is such a big fuss. I feel like a pincushion," Darla finally protested. "Why can't I just wear my hair in the normal pinned up braid?"

Ketzia didn't answer. Her mouth was full of pins.

"Don't you know, dear?" Miss Miranda strode by in her gray traveling dress. "You catch the eye of every man at the show. You are special, and the doctor won't have you wasted."

Heat crept into Darla's cheeks, and her fingers tightened around the handle of her mirror. "I certainly hope that's not the way the doctor really feels. I spent too many years of my life thinking my looks were my only value, and I don't want to feel that way anymore."

Miss Miranda moved to the edge of the campsite, her shoulders rigid. She glanced back at Darla. "Enjoy it while you can, dear. Some day you'll be dried up and unwanted, like an old potato in the bottom of a sack. Just remember this . . . The woman all the men smiled at . . . used to be me." She sauntered off to her tent.

Darla put down the mirror. "What makes her so sour? She's beautiful. And so brave! I could never carry snakes around my neck!"

Ketzia shrugged. "Miss Miranda gets fussy sometimes. She'll be all right tomorrow."

Fatima came by with her sons tumbling behind her, as usual. "Ketizia, can you mind the baby for a moment. I need to give the boys haircuts before we move on."

"Of course." Ketzia spread her shawl over a patch of thick grass, and Fatima placed the baby on the soft, makeshift mattress.

Fatima took a pair of shears from the pile of supplies Ketzia had piled on the rocks. "We'll be back in a little while."

The sun filtered through the trees and settled on the ground in bright, brilliant splotches.

Ketzia held out one of her bracelets to the baby.

The little one grasped the thick metal ring, her eyes growing wide. She put the bracelet in her mouth and cooed.

"They have to taste everything, don't they?" said Darla.

"She's such a sweet baby." Ketzia stroked the soft ebony curls. "It's nice to have a tiny one in the camp. Fatima has kept us in good supply of children to play with." She glanced up at Darla. "Do you like babies?"

"As much as anyone, but I never thought I'd be good at keeping one," said Darla. She rested her chin on her hand. "To tell the truth, I never thought I'd want to marry and settle down, either. Figured no one would want me, due to my chosen profession. But every now and again, I'd hear about a girl who got swept off her feet by some cowboy." She shook her head. "Didn't think there was a man alive who could offer me enough to be a *wife*."

"Ah, but look what could come of it." Ketzia picked up the baby and handed her to Darla.

As the baby snuggled against her shoulder, Darla sighed. *If only.*

Preparations for Waco continued throughout the day. Even while they walked beside the wagons, the troupe polished and mended and practiced.

Despite these distractions, Darla thoughts drifted to Ethan. Part of her hoped he'd discovered the truth. If he despised her, perhaps he could move on with his life. On the other hand, her heart throbbed when she thought of how poorly he must think of her.

Best I don't know. Maybe I was never meant to be a wife, anyway.

When the group stopped for the midday meal, Johnny came to sit by Darla with his bowl of beans. He handed her a hunk of johnnycake. "No molasses left, sorry. Doctor says we'll pick up some in town."

"Oh, that's all right. I like it plain." She nibbled on the bread.

Johnny's blue eyes followed every movement. "Hey, the doctor wants us to think of a new play for the fancy folks. I was thinking about a wedding."

"A wedding? What are you talking about?"

He gave her a sheepish smile. "Well, it would be pretend, you know. But you could sing a song, and wear a dress."

"Silly boy, who would I marry?"

"I don't know . . ." He poked at the ground with a little twig. "How 'bout me?"

"Oh . . . Johnny." Darla resisted the urge to tousle the boy's blond head. His face was so serious she knew it would insult him. "I'm an old woman, and you're such a sweet boy. I don't think we should do a wedding."

"I understand." His jabs to the ground became fiercer. "It was worth a try."

Darla decided to try and change the subject. "Hey Johnny, you know just about everything that goes on around here, don't you?"

He sat up straight, and his chest puffed out a little. "Course I do."

"You have any idea why Miss Miranda told me I wasn't allowed in the lead wagon?"

He frowned. "That's where they keep all the medicines and stuff. I'm not even allowed in there."

"But why not? What are they hiding from us?"

Johnny Jingles shook his head. "You worry too much." He licked the last drops of broth from his dish. "I'm gonna clean out Lucy's pen."

Darla gathered the dishes and took them over to the washbasin. As she scrubbed them clean, the thought kept coming up in her mind, like a bad penny. *What are they hiding from us? What if it's something terrible? I have to find out.*

After she dried the dishes and stacked them in their crate, she walked over to the lead wagon, attempting to keep her eyes forward. *Can't check to see if anyone's watching. I don't want anyone to get suspicious.* Her heart thudded dully in her chest, and her tongue rested like a dried prune in her mouth, though she'd just taken a drink.

No one crossed her path. *Everyone's by the fire. I'll only take a peek. I have to know.*

Darting around the wagon, she leaned against the side, trying to keep her breathing level. She made it to the wagon's little door and rested an ear against the wood. Only silence came from within. The lock wasn't fastened. She reached a trembling hand towards the brass door knob and swung the door open.

Chests and boxes sat on shelves before her, strapped in so they wouldn't crash to the ground when the wagons moved. She climbed up the steps and entered the wagon. A row of green bottles lined the shelf and she picked one up, squinting to read the label. It proved to be in a foreign language. She returned it to its place and walked towards the back of the wagon.

She froze. Three large jars had a shelf to themselves at the end. They were full of a translucent liquid, and each had a different object floating in them.

What could those possibly be? Darla scooted closer and touched one of the jars. A shaft of light fell on the container from the wagon's tiny window. Suddenly it dawned on her and she staggered back. *It's a heart! Maybe even a human heart! And that must be a brain . . . is the third thing a liver?* She slapped her hand over her mouth, trying to hold in her breakfast.

"Just what do you think you're doing?" A woman hissed.

"Oh!" Darla pressed a hand against her chest. "Miss Miranda! I . . . I was looking for you." *Another lie.*

"I don't think so." Miss Miranda's face had gone white except for two bright spots on her cheeks. She grabbed Darla's wrist with surprising strength. "I bet you were trying to steal from us. Folks who've taken you in and cared for you all this time!"

"Steal something? Oh no, of course not!"

Miss Miranda yanked her down the wagon steps. "You know we keep the money in there."

Doctor Ebenezer puffed over from the fire. "Miss Miranda, what is going on over here?"

"I caught her trying to steal money!" Miss Miranda pulled Darla forward. "She was in the lead wagon, after I strictly forbid her to go in there."

Doctor Ebenezer's mustache trembled. "Is this true, Darla?"

Tears ran down Darla's cheeks. "No. I would never steal from you! I was just . . . curious, that's all. I thought maybe . . . you were hiding something."

Other members of the troupe gathered around the wagon. Darla caught Ketzia's worried stare and looked away.

"What you're saying is, you didn't trust us." Doctor Ebenezer's tone was grave.

Darla lifted her chin. "And for good reason! Why do you have those body parts, anyway? Are you practicing some kind of magic arts?"

"No, Darla," the doctor said quietly. "Those are medical specimens I have purchased over the years for study. I don't show them to new troupe members right away for this very reason. I don't want to frighten anyone."

"Oh." Darla looked down at the ground. *Of course they are medical specimens. Why didn't I think of that? I was so sure there would be something bad.*

The Doctor took her hand and looked up into her face. Darla almost felt he was trying to read her very soul. "I will ask you once more. Were you planning to steal from me, and all of your friends, here?"

Darla drew herself up. "Never."

He blinked and turned to the rest of the group. "I believe this woman. Curiosity killed the cat, but it does not mean she's a thief. Everyone go back to work, please. Let's not have another word about it."

Miss Miranda's mouth dropped open, and she looked as though she wanted to say a great many things. Instead she turned and went into the wagon, slamming the door behind her.

The other troupe members turned and walked away, including Ketzia. The gypsy girl's head was bowed.

"Thank you," Darla said to Doctor Ebenezer.

Doctor Ebenezer's shoulders sagged, and he looked much older than ever before. "Perhaps someday, Miss North, you will believe in me."

20

Caring for Jack

Two miles from Willoughby, Jack's gait shifted. Though the change was slight, years of riding had taught Ethan not to ignore the sensation. "Whoa. Whoa, boy." He stopped the horse and dismounted.

Tying the reins to a nearby elm tree, he used a stick to clean out the right front hoof. All of Jack's shoes had looked fine last night. There had been no loose nails or gaps. Ethan dug deeper into the hollow, flicking out mud. No big rocks or thorns. *There.* Almost too small to see. A pea-sized pocket of pus.

"Oh, Jack, I can't drain it here. Let's try to make it into town and see if we can get you some help." Ethan kicked at a glop of mud. The road had been damp for most of the journey. A situation like this wasn't surprising, even though he'd been careful to clean Jack's hooves every time they stopped.

He started to remount, then shook his head. *Better not. It's not that far to town anyway.*

An hour later, he reached the town of Hamilton. Long shadows lined the streets from houses on the sides. Dogs barked at him, and housewives shopping for last-minute supper items hurried past.

An inquiry and a pointed arm led him to a boarding house, next to a saloon. He tied Jack to the hitching post. When he pushed on the ancient, half-rotted door, it creaked open on leather hinges. The sharp scent of mildew and rot filled his nose and tickled his tongue. *Wish I'd brought in my canteen.*

An old woman sat on a stool. She leaned against a wall, looking through a catalogue.

After eyeing the peeled wallpaper and stained floor, Ethan sighed. *It's not like I have a choice.* "Could I please have a room for the night?"

She looked him up and down, and a smirk tugged at her wizened lips. "With or without companionship?"

Heat rose to his face. "Oh, gosh. Without, please. I will need a stall for my horse, a place where I can fix a bad hoof."

Opening her catalogue again, she waved a dismissive hand. "It'll be a quarter for the room and a dime more for the stall. You might find some tools in the stable, if the last lout didn't take off with 'em."

"Thank you kindly." Ethan placed the money on the counter and tipped his hat, though the gesture went unnoticed.

Piles of manure and puddles of mud filled most of the vacant stalls. Ethan sighed. *Better to sell Jack to a knacker now than let him stay in this place the way it is.* He spent over an hour cleaning out the least disgusting stall and spread out several layers of straw from a pile behind the stable.

After leading his horse into the dark building, Ethan managed to find a hoof-pick and a bottle of liniment. His nose wrinkled when he pulled out the cork. "Something that smells that bad must be powerful stuff, Jack."

Jack snorted and turned his head.

With experienced hands, Ethan cleaned the hoof and drained the pus. He made a poultice from the liniment and moss he'd picked up in the woods. *Darla could be in this town right now and I might miss her again.* His hands shook as he re-corked the bottle. *I just don't think I could stand it.* But he knew better than to ignore his horse's malady. Folks had lost perfectly good mounts from far less serious ailments.

An hour later, he left the stable and walked down the town's dusty little streets, scanning walls and fences for handbills. Scoundrels scowled at him from wanted posters, and advertisements for remedies screamed for his attention. He saw nothing about Doctor Ebenezer.

He counted days in his head. Could he have passed the caravan somehow without realizing it? No, he had taken the only road the large wagons could safely pass. He couldn't have missed them.

A young girl hurried by with a basket of eggs.

"Hey there, Miss." He touched her shoulder. "Did a medicine show pass through here?"

The girl looked him over with a wary eye. "Yes," she stammered. "About two days ago."

Pulling off his hat, Ethan ran a hand through his hair while the child scurried off. *Could I have missed it? Could the man in the last town have been wrong about the dates?*

At the post office he found what he'd been searching for. A handbill, held by one corner. "Professor Ingleburt's Marvels." *A different show.*

Darla's group must have gone somewhere else. He staggered back against the post. The troupe could have gone in any direction. With a partially lame horse, there was no sense even trying to figure out where.

Ethan sank against the wall. *Such a foolish journey. I wasted money better spent for other things. I left my mother to struggle with Downs House on her own. And I followed after a girl who wouldn't have left in the first place if she cared for me.*

A tiny flame burned in his heart, carrying a message in a flickering light. *What if she does care, just as Sarah cared.*

He couldn't bear the thought of being responsible for leaving another woman alone in her sadness. *I must bear it. I've done everything I can.*

Catching sight of his reflection in a shop window, he grimaced. No wonder the little girl had looked so alarmed. Curls tumbled from beneath his hat, and scraggly hairs stuck out from his beard like rusted wires. He hadn't had a bath since he'd left the Duncan's home.

Ethan returned to the boarding house steps, paused and counted his money. Sighing, he went back inside and stood at the counter. He waited for the woman to look up from the catalogue she still read.

"Do you have a bath house here?" he asked.

"Sure do, mister. Soap's extra. If you want, I'll throw in a hair cut and a shave by my husband out yonder. Everything for ten cents."

Ethan handed the woman another precious dime and pushed his way into the second room, where he was greeted by a rusty wash basin and an ancient scrub-brush with half the bristles missing.

He was about to pull off his shirt when the woman walked in without knocking. She handed him a soft hunk of homemade soap and a none-too-clean flour sack.

"Thanks," said Ethan.

"Hmm hmmm." She went out the door.

Ethan plunged his arm in the icy water, where the soap dissolved into tiny useless bits that floated on the surface. He stared at them and shook his head.

Yes. Tomorrow I'll head for home.

*"Johnson City,
Johnson City,
Where all the girls
Are so pretty"*

Johnny sang in time to the jingling of his shoes.

"Aren't you a little young to be thinking about pretty girls?" Darla teased.

"Yes, but it's a nice little ditty," Johnny sang. He glanced over at Darla. "Besides, none of the ladies there will be prettier than you and Mrs. Ketzia."

"Why, Master Jingles, you're making me blush," said Darla, making a show of covering her cheeks with her hands.

After the incident with the lead wagon, most of the troupe had avoided her. She didn't blame them. It made sense they would believe Miss Miranda over a newcomer. She'd spent last night rolled up in a blanket by the campfire, alone.

The hardest was Ketzia, who hadn't said much, only looked at her with sorrowful eyes. Darla's only friend now was Johnny, who pretended as though nothing had happened at all.

"Are you finished, with your chores, Johnny?" Miss Miranda's sharp voice interrupted Darla's thoughts. She stood behind them, hands on her hips, eyebrows drawn to her nose in a fierce point. "Make sure you feed the snakes today. I don't want them fractious."

"Yes, Ma'am. I'll check the traps." Johnny Jingles tipped his hat and ran off towards the woods.

"Darla." Miss Miranda gave her a rare smile. "I have a favor to ask of you?"

"Me?" The snake charmer hadn't spoken to Darla since yesterday, and the looks she'd shot her when they did meet could have killed a rat.

"Doctor Ebenezer wants you to run into the town nearby and pick up a packet of hairpins and some ribbons. He wants all of us ladies to match in Waco. I think blue would be nice, don't you?"

"Even Ketzia and Fatima?" Darla had never seen the gypsy women wear anything in their hair but scarves.

"Yes, yes, of course." Miss Miranda handed her a dime. "This town is small, but the general store should have what we need. Just be quick about it." She pointed through the trees. "Follow that path. Should take you less than twenty minutes to run the errand. We'll be here for at least another hour."

"Shouldn't I see if someone can go along?" Darla glanced around. Ketzia was grooming the horses, but Darla couldn't bear to face her friend's sad smile today.

Surely we have enough ribbons. But she was familiar with Doctor Ebenezer's eccentricities, and he'd been very particular in his preparations for Waco. He'd even told Johnny to polish the snakes. Darla looked after Miss Miranda's departing figure and bit her lip. *I'm certainly not in a position to protest. I'll go and not complain about it.*

The sun had burned through the gray clouds at last, and bright new wildflowers dotted the sides of the path, including Darla's favorites, the flaming red Indian Paintbrushes. As a child, she'd always thought the cold of

192

winter would never go away. But every year spring unfurled like a dress with brilliant patterns in every fold.

True to Miss Miranda's word, houses soon appeared through the trees. The town consisted of a few staggered buildings, plain without the bother of false fronts, built around a main street. No one walked the dusty roads.

A creaking noise came from a building near the end of the block. When Darla walked closer, she saw a battered sign that read "General Store" hanging by a rusted wire. The breeze hit the sign, and it squeaked again.

Darla crept up the sagging steps. The door was open a crack, and she pushed into the dark, dusty room.

The area behind the counter was empty. No sounds of movement came from behind a dingy curtain she assumed led to the back area. Boxes and bags of food were piled in haphazard fashion on the shelves around her, along with gardening tools, packets of needles, and other dry goods. She didn't see any ribbons. *Why had Miss Miranda been so sure this tiny little store would have them?*

After taking one last look around, Darla stepped out onto the porch. "Hello?" she called.

"Hello, Miss." A tall, thin man stood at the end of the porch. He wore a threadbare suit that might have been dapper years before. A faded stovepipe hat rested on his head. His lip curled up over yellowed teeth. "Can I help you?"

"Yes." Darla flashed him her brightest smile. "I'm searching for hair ribbons ... blue ones."

"Is that so?" The man stalked past her and into the shop, his worn but polished shoes squeaking with every step. He had a curious way of walking, with his elbows pointed out at the sides, like a scarecrow being jerked by an errant wind.

The hairs on the back of Darla's neck pricked up. *You're being silly. Everything's fine.* She followed the man back into the shop.

"Folks around these parts don't hold much with frippery," the man said. He rummaged through a box on the counter. "Here. These ribbons'll do you fine. Two for a penny."

Darla touched one of the stiff strips of fabric gingerly. "Sir, I'm sorry, but I need blue ribbons. These are black."

The man leered at her. "So, these ribbons ain't good enough for your hoity-toity hair? Well, you can just get out of my shop if you're not gonna buy."

A hot retort sprang to Darla's mind. She thought better of it, turned on her heel, and went back out into the street.

A group of women, all dressed in black mourning garb, huddled together at the far end of the road. Three gentlemen laughed and talked in front of the store. Darla hurried past them, intent on returning to the caravan. How long had she been gone? At least half an hour, by the sun's position. She walked faster.

A flurry of bright skirts caught her eye, further on at the edge of town.

Ketzia? What on earth? She ran towards her friend.

Ketzia's warm brown cheeks were tinged with red, and sweat beaded her forehead.

"Darla," she gasped. "Why are you here?"

"Miss Miranda sent me for ribbons. She said Doctor Ebenezer wanted me to fetch some. Surely she told you?"

Ketzia pursed her lips. "No. The doctor was looking for you. Miss Miranda told him you stormed off after saying medicine show life wasn't for you. But I saw her hide your things in the bushes. Darla, I'm so sorry, I should have known you were telling the truth!"

Darla sighed. "What am I going to do? If Miss Miranda hates me so much she'd try to get rid of me like this, I'll never be safe in the show." She lifted her chin. "Look, thank you for coming to tell me. But I'd better find somewhere else to go. I'll wait until the caravan leaves and go pull my stuff out of the bushes. You have been a wonderful friend to me. Tell Doctor Ebenezer I . . . I'm sorry."

Ketzia folded her arms. "I refuse to let you go off alone. You shouldn't have even come to town by yourself, and Miss Miranda knew it. You need to come and tell Doctor Ebenezer the truth about her. I'll back you up."

Voices behind Darla grew louder, and Ketzia craned her neck over Darla's head.

Darla whirled around to see crowds of people stopping on the street, pointing to them. Goosebumps rose on her skin.

Ketzia leaned closer. "Listen," she said in a low voice, "we found the town's message tree this morning while you were out with Johnny. Seems they don't like outsiders. You should come with us, at least until we reach Waco."

Darla opened her mouth to argue, but out of the corner of her eye she saw the shopkeeper leading a group of people towards them.

The gypsy girl tugged on her arm. "Hurry!" she hissed. "I have a horse tied up right beyond those trees. I told my brothers we'd catch up. The caravan already left."

Picking up her skirts, Darla hastened after her, but gravel crunched behind them, closer and closer. Her heart sank as they turned to face the crowd, which had grown to more than a dozen men and women.

"Can we help you?" She tried to give a confident smile, with just a dash of sass.

"This foreign girl a friend of yours?" the shopkeeper demanded.

"Why yes," Darla replied in as cool a tone as she could muster. "Is there a problem?"

A thin woman with sunken cheeks stepped forward. "Caravan came through here afore Christmas. Sold my sister Marge an elixir for constipation. And she was dead afore the New Year."

"That's right," another woman nodded. "And they had gypsies, like you." She pointed to Ketzia. "They had all kinda magical powers. They put curses on the town."

"Curses . . . on the town?" Darla's throat tightened.

The shopkeeper jabbed a spindly finger at her. "This girl was in my store stirring up trouble."

Darla's fingers clenched into fists. "I was just looking for blue hair ribbons!" She stomped her foot.

The crowd gasped.

The woman in black shook her fist. "Wasn't blue the color worn by those gypsies the last time?

Cries of "Yes, yes it was!" came from other people on the street.

Heart pounding, Darla looked for a gap in the crowd, but she and Ketzia were surrounded.

Two men grabbed Ketzia and two more took Darla's elbows. She struggled and kicked. "You have no right to touch us!"

Ketzia's eyes were wide, and she chewed her lip.

Darla slouched down between her captors. Thick fingers dug into her arms.

The men dragged them down the street, everyone else following behind.

The shopkeeper stepped before the throng, and they all stopped. "Where should we take these two troublemakers until the sheriff gets back? We can't get into the jail 'till the law arrives."

The thin woman pointed over to a side street. "Take 'em to my shed. It's got good strong walls and a lock." She bent towards Ketzia. "You'll be punished for what your people did to my sister. Make no mistake about that."

"My family has never even been to this town!" Ketzia's shawl had slipped down her back and her wild, black hair whipped in the wind. "Dozens of medicine shows go through Texas every year. My family doesn't practice black magic. Magic is from the Devil!"

A man reached out and slapped Ketzia across the face. "You will not speak of the Devil in this town, pagan creature!"

Ketzia's fingers crept to her cheek. Her eyes blazed, but she kept silent.

Tears burned Darla's eyes. *Oh, what can we do?* Even if the folks from the caravan tried to rescue them, they would be outnumbered.

They were taken to a little house on the outskirts of town. The cottage was painted a light green with white trim, and cheerful petunias nodded out front.

How could such a horrible woman live in such a beautiful house? This thought was swept from Darla's mind as she was grabbed by the shoulders and shoved towards a small shed. The door yawned open, like a mouth ready to swallow her whole.

Darla clasped her hands in front of her. "Please don't do this. We've done nothing wrong."

"That'll be for Sheriff Doyle to decide," said the lady in black.

Darla was pushed into the shed, and Ketzia followed. The door slammed shut, and a bolt rasped into place.

Pounding on the door, Darla screamed, "You can't keep us in here! You have no right!"

"Be quiet there!" a rough man's voice answered.

Thin cracks in the walls let in needles of light, the only relief from the darkness. The shed was mostly empty, with just a few boxes and bags in a corner.

Ketzia stood and began rummaging through them. "Nothing useful." She sat against the wall and crossed her arms.

"What should we do?" Darla tried to push down the panic rising in her voice. *Even if we found a way out, there's a guard.*

But Ketzia had bowed her head and was praying in a language Darla couldn't understand. *Probably Russian, or perhaps a gypsy tongue.*

Darla couldn't think of words to speak. Fear and desperation fought inside her mind, and she wanted to slam against the wall and scream.

She clenched her hands and sank to her knees. "Jesus, Jesus, Jesus," she prayed, over and over. Finally she quieted, and allowed the Holy Spirit to pour into her. Something in her heart shifted, and a peace flooded through her soul. Immediately, she felt the presence of God surround her. Her hand slipped up, up into the air, almost on its own.

Everything is going to be all right. The certainty of this thought pressed out every trace of fear within her.

Her eyes fluttered open, and she met Ketzia's gaze.

Ketzia smiled. "He told you, too."

"Maybe there's a loose board somewhere." Darla began to test the walls with her shoulder. "We can't just give up. Maybe the guard will leave, and we can escape tonight."

A shadow covered a space where light had just been visible. Ragged breaths sounded from the other side of the wall

21

Charter Morgan

"Darla, is that you? Are you all right?" came a husky whisper.

All at once, Darla had the sensation she was stepping back into that Christmas fairyland she had created for the orphan's banquet. Lights danced before her eyes, and she patted her cheeks. *Am I dreaming?* Yes, this must be a dream, because dreams were the only places she heard Ethan's voice.

"Oh Ethan." She leaned against the wall. "Why must you torment me? Please go away."

"Go away?" the voice said. "Shouldn't I rescue you first?"

The door groaned and was wrenched it from its hinges. Light poured into the shed.

"Ethan, it *is* you!" Darla ran forward and threw her arms around his neck.

"Shhh . . ." Ethan stared down at her, a hundred questions burning in his eyes. "I let the chickens out to distract the guard. He'll be back any time."

Darla pulled away, heat rising to her cheeks. "I'm sorry," she whispered. "It's . . . good to be rescued."

"Come on, Darla." Ketzia was already moving past them. "I left my horse on the other side of town. We'll have to skirt around through the woods."

"Hey, those girls have to stay here!" The guard stomped in their direction, his face like a swollen tomato, sweat pouring down red cheeks.

Darla was all for taking a chance and running, but Ketzia grabbed her arm and nodded to a gun holster on the guard's hip.

Ethan turned and waited for the burly man. "Did you have something to say to me?"

The guard squinted at him. "Uh, yeah. It's my job to make sure these ladies stay put until the law arrives."

"Is that so?" Ethan stepped closer. "I'm sure a smart-looking fellow like yourself can tell me just what these girls did wrong."

"We didn't do anything!" said Darla. "And he knows it!"

The guard cracked his knuckles and swaggered forward until he was inches from Ethan's face.

The two men stared at each other. Ethan seemed calm, his shoulders relaxed. The guard's shoulders heaved with each breath.

Darla didn't want to think about what that breath must smell like, but Ethan didn't seem to be affected. "I'm taking these ladies with me, and you're not going to stop me."

The guard's fingers twitched over his holster, and Darla screamed out. "Ethan!"

Ethan swung his arm back so fast Darla almost missed the motion. His fist connected with the guard's jaw in a crunch Darla felt in her very core. The guard crumpled to the ground.

"Shall we, ladies?" Ethan flexed the fingers of his right hand and nodded to the forest.

Bushes embraced them in leafy boughs. In a few steps, the town was covered.

It didn't take long to skirt the small group of houses. Ketzia beckoned to them. "I left my horse over here."

Men's laughter rang through the trees. The shopkeeper stood in the clearing with a group of his cronies, holding the horse's bridle.

"What should we do?" Darla whispered to Ketzia, but Ethan was already pulling them into the clearing.

The shopkeeper's mouth dropped open, but then a slow smile spread across his face. "Hey, boys, lookee here. Thought they'd get away, didn't they?"

"How dare you?" Ethan clenched his fists and stalked forward.

"Blondie's friends with that witch girl." A pudgy man in coveralls pointed to Ketzia. "Said she was bringing the Devil to our town."

"Ketzia said no such thing!" Darla protested.

Ethan raised his hands. "Folks, why don't we discuss this like gentlemen?" He pulled a paper from his pocket and began to unfold it. "My name is Ethan Downs. I'm part of a large church group in Dallas. And Darla North," he took Darla's hand, "is with me."

The shopkeeper took the paper and examined it. "You don't say." He handed it back to Ethan. "A preacher, eh?"

"Of sorts. And I can tell you right now, this young lady," he indicated Ketzia, "wouldn't have to bring the Devil to your town. He's been allowed to create plenty of mischief all by his lonesome." He glowered at each man in the group. "Hasn't he, gentlemen?"

A beak-nosed man stared at Darla's arms.

Probably trying to figure out if I have bruises where he grabbed me. She gave him a slit-eyed glare.

The shopkeeper scuffed the ground with a booted toe. "You and your woman are free to go. But we'll have to keep this foreign girl for questioning."

Ethan stepped closer. "You will hand me those reins, sir, and both of these ladies and I will take our leave. Now."

"And who's gonna make us?" the shopkeeper taunted.

Ethan stared down at the broken skin on his knuckles. "Charter Morgan."

"Eh?" coverall man asked.

"Ask him," Ethan pointed to the shopkeeper, whose shoulders had slumped. "Charter Morgan is the charitable organization I work with. They buy a great portion of your corn and potato crops here, through this shopkeeper. Don't they?" This last question was addressed to the shopkeeper.

Pride filled Darla's heart. *Ethan is magnificent.*

The shopkeeper rolled his eyes heavenward and sighed. He slapped the reins into Ethan's hands and stalked away. The other men followed him back towards the town.

Ethan watched as they left. "Cowards," he muttered.

"Ethan, I declare, it's almost as though you wish they'd stayed to fight," said Darla.

"No." Ethan tugged at his shirt sleeves, unbuttoned them and rolled them up. "I don't know anymore."

Ketzia glanced from Ethan to Darla and pursed her lips. "The caravan won't be far. Mr. Downs, do you have a horse?"

"He couldn't go any further." Ethan bowed his head. "The reason I stopped here in the first place."

"It's all right, we'll hurry and catch up." Ketzia grabbed the horse's reins and led him down the path. "Let's stop at the camp and get your things," she said over her shoulder to Darla.

Ethan and Darla followed behind.

Warmth crept to Darla's cheeks and she stole sidelong glances at Ethan, but he stared straight ahead into the woods as they walked, saying nothing.

Finally she could no longer bear the silence.

"You came all this way for me?" she asked in a timid voice.

"No. Not all this way." He glanced at her. "Only to Hamilton. But you weren't there. So I decided to head for Waco and catch a train home. Jack's leg wasn't holding up like I hoped it would. He needed rest. I sold him in that town. I was on my way out when I saw the commotion in the street."

"You saw that? Why didn't you step in right away?"

Ethan rubbed his chin. "I couldn't very well have taken on the whole crowd, could I? No, better to wait and see what happened. I saw the Charter Morgan sign on the shop door. I remembered their connection with my organization. Then I had the leverage, see?"

"That makes sense." Darla sighed. "Well, you're here now, and we're rescued."

"Yep."

Darla studied his face for a hint of softening, but he stared ahead at the path with steely eyes. She held her hands tightly together to keep from wringing them. *Oh dear,*

dear. Somehow, he really found me and rescued me, but everything is awful. Why did he come after me if he was so upset?

Ketzia stopped when they reached the clearing where the caravan had camped. She reached down behind a log and pulled out Darla's bag, covered in twigs and moss. "Here you are." She handed it to Darla.

"The caravan went this way." Tugging on the horse's reins, Ketzia continued down the path.

Birds sang from the treetops in praise of the sun and spring, and a creek bubbled over the rocks not far away. Ethan marched a step ahead of Darla, and she almost had to run to keep up with his long strides. Suddenly his shoulders squared and he stopped. "Hey, Darla."

"Yes, Ethan?"

"Is he there? At the caravan?"

"Who?"

"That Jethro man. Why'd he let you go into town by yourself?"

Realization flooded over Darla like a spark from a tinderbox. "Ethan Downs, you thought I ran away with that . . . toad of a man! Why, never in my life . . ." Her knees buckled, and she took a deep breath to steady herself.

He inhaled sharply and swung around. "Well then, why'd you go? I guess it's pretty pathetic, but I rode all over the Texas countryside looking for you. Thought you and I . . . well, I thought there was . . ."

She put an arm on his shoulder, and he stopped. "We were. I mean, there was."

Ketzia swung around. "You two want to be lost out here? We have to keep moving."

"Why don't you ride on ahead and tell the caravan to wait for us?" Darla suggested.

"Are you sure you'll be all right?"

Darla nodded. "We'll be fine."

Ketzia grabbed a handful of the black pony's mane and jumped on its back. Her hair billowed around her shoulders as the horse thundered down the path.

"What interesting people you've met." Ethan stared after her.

"Hmmm. Yes, I have met some great folks." Darla scuffed last fall's leaves as she walked, watching them rise and fall over her shoes. "Ethan, why did you come after me?"

"No." He swung around. "I asked you a question first." Pain and sorrow glinted in his eyes.

"Oh Ethan . . ." Tears slipped down Darla's cheeks. She dabbed at them with her sleeve. "I knew you would find out about my past, and I couldn't bear it."

"Is that what this was all about?" Ethan gulped. "The place you came from?"

"Yes." Darla tried to swallow her sobs, a task she knew would soon be impossible.

"Darla," Ethan cupped her cheek with a strong, gentle hand, "I know all about your past. Brother Jenkins told us your history when he asked if you could stay at Downs House."

"You knew?" Darla gasped. "And Ma Downs knew?" Her voice sank to a whisper. "And you accepted me anyway?"

"Of course I did." Ethan took her hands. "We've all done things we're not proud of. I've done plenty, even though I've tried to serve Jesus all my life. You gave your heart to God. You are a changed person. If God doesn't hold it against you, why should I?"

"There aren't many folks who would think that way."

"But it's the right way." Ethan bent closer and tucked a curl behind Darla's ear.

"What did your mother think, you coming all the way out here and leaving the ministry behind?"

"Ma sent me with her blessing. She knew I'd never find such a sweet, kind, beautiful girl anywhere else. She's a good judge of character." Ethan searched Darla's eyes. "So, what do you say, Darla? Will you be my wife?"

Darla's breath caught in her throat. "Are you sure?" she managed to choke.

Ethan chuckled. "I've rambled in the woods, slept on the ground, rode a lame horse and eaten nothing but beans, hard bread and salt pork for days. And somehow, only God knows how, I found you." His eyebrows drew together. "I've never been so sure of anything in my life."

Something broke inside of Darla, the thick shell of sadness that had held her heart captive for these weeks on the road. Bubbles of joy welled up within her, and she threw her arms around Ethan. "Of course I'll marry you!"

The honey-sawdust scent surrounded her, and he wrapped her in his arms. His kisses were warm and sweet, the kind she'd been waiting for all her life.

For the first time since her father's death, Darla felt love flowing from another person's touch. Love, acceptance and protection.

"Halloo?" came a voice through the trees.

Darla reluctantly pulled away. "Doctor Ebenezer?"

The doctor pushed through the underbrush. "Darla, are you all right?" His eyebrows shot up when he saw Ethan. "When I found out Ketzia was gone, I made everyone stop. I was just about to send her brothers out to look for her when she rode up. She told us everything." He grinned at Ethan. "So, this must be your young man?"

"Yes, this is my young man." Darla squeezed Ethan's hand. "Ethan Downs, meet Doctor Ebenezer."

The doctor shook Ethan's hand. "Please to meet you, sir." He pointed to the carpenter's scars on Ethan's palm. "I got a liniment that will make those disappear right away."

"I'm sure you do." Ethan stuck his hand into a pocket.

Doctor Ebenezer turned to Darla. "Ketzia told me what Miranda tried to do. The woman can get jealous, but I can assure you she didn't realize the people of the town would try to harm you."

Darla frowned. "I'll take your word for it. But she won't have to share the spotlight anymore, anyway."

"I assume you'll be taking off with your young man, here?"

Darla slipped her hand into the crook of Ethan's elbow. "Yes, Sir. I will miss you all very much."

The doctor grinned. "If you ever change your mind--" He darted a glance at Ethan. "No, I don't suppose you will."

They arrived in the clearing. All the men came and welcomed Ethan with handshakes and slaps on the back. Fatima gave Darla a tight hug. Johnny Jingles smiled when he saw her, but his face clouded over when she introduced Ethan. Miss Miranda was nowhere in sight.

"Sulking in the lead wagon," Ketzia whispered to Darla.

The caravan began to move again, and Ethan and Darla walked hand in hand in their wake, talking over the last week's adventures.

22

Home at Last

The evening's moon rose clear and round, spilling light over the wagons. Ketzia's family brought out their instruments, and the troupe danced by the fire.

Darla danced with Ethan, then Johnny Jingles, then Doctor Ebenezer, then Ethan again.

"I finally get to dance with you." Ethan grabbed her hands and twirled her over the field. She threw her head back to see the stars spinning above her, as though they shared her joy.

The zanies pulled out the best of the provisions, and everyone, except for Ketzia's family, dined on pickled beets, roast venison, and peach cobbler cooked in a Dutch oven.

After supper the music started up again. Ethan raised his eyebrows and nodded towards the dancers, but Darla shook her head. Her feet burned from dancing.

She scooted closer to Ethan's place on the log they were sharing. "I wish this night could last forever."

"It has been nice," Ethan put his arm around her. "But I want to marry you pretty quick, and Ma would never forgive us if we didn't invite her to the wedding."

"Neither would Lisbeth." Darla snuggled against his shoulder. She could scarcely believe that only six months ago, her home had been a saloon where she was used and mistreated every day by men who only saw her as a plaything. *It's been so hard, but I'm so thankful for the journey.*

"Now, let's talk practical for a moment," said Ethan, drawing her hands up under his chin. "Since I had to sell Jack, I planned to take the train back to Dallas. I looked over my money, and I'll have just enough for two tickets."

"I have money, too." Darla drew out a little pouch, which contained money she'd saved and her week's earnings. "I'm sorry you had to sell your horse."

"Me too." Ethan stared into the fire. "Hopefully the townsfolk treat their horses better than ex-saloon girls." His mouth curled into a smile.

"Ethan, don't be mean!"

She traced his jaw with her finger, the day-old whiskers feeling just as she'd imagined they would. "You never told me . . . why you decided to come after me."

Ethan's face fell. "Because once upon a time, I didn't go after someone else."

"Sarah?"

Ethan glanced up. "Someone told you about her?"

"Just that she left you right before your wedding. They didn't know everything that happened."

"No one else knows the whole story but Ma." Ethan pulled a crumpled piece of paper from his duster pocket and smoothed it over his knee. It was too dim to read in the firelight, but he wasn't looking at the page anyway.

"It says, 'Dear Mr. Downs. I am writing you at the request of a Miss Sarah Blake. I regret to inform you this was her last request. Three days ago, she passed away from complications of tuberculosis. With Deepest Regrets, Anne Hodge, Fair Ridge Sanitarium.'"

Darla stared out over the flames and into the night. Most of the troupe had already left the fire to finish the last evening tasks. The music of the crickets replaced the gypsies' wild song. "I'm so sorry," she managed to say.

Ethan crumpled the paper and placed it in her hand. "I kept this for two years to remind myself. If I ever felt that way about someone again, I'd never let them go. My heart was filled with so much pride, Darla. At the time, the notion she had another reason, that she was trying to spare me some great pain, never entered my mind. This time . . . I needed to know why." He touched her cheek. "To hear it from those beautiful lips."

"Ethan, I'm so sorry. I should have trusted you."

He twined his fingers through hers. "Do you believe me now?"

"With all my heart."

The next morning was a bittersweet blur. The great metal bridge leading to Waco rose up over the horizon an hour after breaking camp, and the troupe stopped at the road leading to the structure.

The zanies pulled together their supplies, preparing to head into town and publicize the show.

"Railroad station can't be far from here." Ethan shaded his eyes and squinted towards the bridge. "Darla, you and I should probably go and try to find the place."

Darla nodded. "I'll be glad to get home." *Home. Do I truly have a real home again?*

Miranda had avoided Darla since she'd returned to camp, and when their paths crossed, she'd turn and walk the other way.

Ketzia slipped Darla a piece of paper. "Here's the address for the ranch where my husband works. If you send me letters there, he'll get them to me when I visit him. I'll write you back and tell all about everything going on with the show."

Darla hugged Ketzia. "Of course we'll stay in touch. I wish you could meet my friend, Soonie. The two of you are both so strong and brave. I'll miss you every day."

Johnny tugged on Darla's sleeve and handed her a creased photograph. "It's me an' Lucy. We'll miss you."

Darla rumpled Johnny's hair one last time. "You keep studying with Doctor Ebenezer, and someday you'll run the show."

Doctor Ebenezer clapped him on the shoulder. "Couldn't do it without him."

Johnny's chest puffed out. "You sure you can't just wait for me instead of marrying Mr. Downs?" he asked, his eyes hopeful.

"Oh Johnny, I'll be old and gray by the time you want to go courting," said Darla.

"No you won't." Johnny grinned. "You'll always be purty, Miss Darla."

"Sorry, kid. I've gone through too much looking for this woman to give her up." Ethan picked up Darla's traveling bag and offered his elbow.

Darla slipped her hand around his arm, savoring the familiar texture of the duster jacket. She followed Ethan across the giant metal bridge.

After a few inquiries, they found the station. A short time later, they boarded the train to Dallas.

Though Darla had looked forward to spending the ride home discussing their new life and plans with Ethan, she ended up falling asleep on his shoulder. She awoke, hours later, as the train pulled into the Dallas depot.

Again they chose to walk the short distance to Downs House.

Darla's pulse quickened when the old building appeared through the trees. Though the place was dilapidated, true, loving people lived there. Pride swelled inside of her. *They consider me family.*

Ma Downs stepped out to the porch and looked towards the road, shading her eyes. When she caught sight of them, she clasped her hands together and rushed down the stairs.

"Ethan, you're home!" Her bonnet fell down her back, and gray hair flew around her face in a tangle.

"Yes. And you can see I found my girl." Ethan took Darla's hand. "Ma, I'd like you to meet my fiancée."

Ma Down's eyes actually sparkled. "I'm glad you waited until you reached home. The ladies would have been so disappointed if they couldn't put on a wedding."

"We can have it here, at Downs House," said Ethan.

"Oh, could we get married in the gazebo?" Darla could already picture the beautiful place, decked in garlands of flowers.

Ma's face paled. She fumbled in her pocket for a handkerchief and dabbed at her brow. "What am I saying? I completely forgot the news. We have lost our main benefactors. The Bugles have withdrawn their support."

"That Samantha," Darla muttered.

"We will have to sell Downs House," Ma Downs continued. "And I don't know where we shall go."

Ethan's forehead wrinkled. "We'll figure out something. We always do. God provides."

Lisbeth came out on the porch and gave Darla a hug. "Glad to see you used the good sense God gave you and came home. What'd you run off for anyway?"

"I'll tell you everything." Darla patted her hand. "Let me get inside and settled first."

Patience stood in the hall as they entered, her hands clasped together. "Oh, you're home! I am glad, Miss Fancy!"

Darla squeezed the little girl's hand. "So am I, Patience. And I can't wait to see what you've painted since I left."

After an evening of stories swapped and delicious food from Miss Betty, Darla went upstairs.

I'm happy they didn't find someone else to take my place. She touched the brilliant pattern of the quilt on her bed, created by Lisbeth's busy fingers. Suddenly, she remembered the bundles of scarves Ketzia and Fatima had taken into towns to sell. Something Doctor Ebenezer had said flickered into her mind. "Folks'll buy anything if you present it in the right way."

She stared at the cloth. "Lisbeth, I think I have an idea that could save Downs House."

Two weeks later, Darla poked her head into the parlor. The room was strewn with fabrics, paper and busy women. Indigo pieced together bonnets, while Marnie knitted scarves as fast as her fingers could fly. Patience painted miniatures at the piano and Ms. Brodie cut out quilt squares.

"Good news, girls," said Darla. "The shopkeeper has given me an order for two dozen bonnets and six more paintings. Seems like the tourists snap them up as fast as he stocks the shelves. And the furniture shop is keeping Ethan so busy he might have to bring in hired help."

"Looks like someone wants a colored girl's pictures after all." Patience held up the painting of a brilliant sunflower she'd just finished.

"Of course they do." Lisbeth held out her hand and let Danny climb up her shoulder, where he regarded them all like a tiny monarch on a throne. "Just like they want an Irish girl's quilts."

Ma Downs stopped Darla in the hall. "I've been working on the receipts, and though I'm remaining cautious, I believe the funds brought in by last weekend's market sales will match what the Bugles provided. If we can keep this going, we might be all right, and even have a bit for each woman to keep for herself."

"And we didn't even have anything of Ethan's to sell yet!" Darla clasped her hands together. "It ought to be better next time, and with the fair coming in September . . . all will be well."

"While I was upstairs looking for quilt scraps, I found this. I was so happy the moths didn't get to it." Ma Downs unrolled a bundle of filmy lace, delicate as frost on a windowpane. "This was my wedding veil. I would like for you to wear it, if you'd like."

Darla gasped and stroked the beautiful fabric with a trembling finger. "It's lovely, Ma Downs. I don't know how to thank you."

Ma Downs patted her hand. "Child, I thank God every day that you walked into my home, and that He helped me see how special you were. He's given you the ability to see the best in people. You coax out dreams and talents they never knew they had. You have brought hope into this home again."

"It was all because *you* chose to see more than a saloon girl," Darla said softly.

The older woman wiped her eyes. "I'll just put this in your room." She gathered up the lace in a snowy cloud.

Darla stepped down the porch and hurried to the workshop. The banging of a hammer greeted her ears.

Golden sheets of light poured through the barn door, and settled on a man's bent figure.

Ethan looked up from his work, and the smile she knew belonged only to her spread across his face. "Hey there, Darla."

About the Author

Angela Castillo has lived in Bastrop, Texas, home of the River Girl, almost her entire life. She studied Practical Theology at Christ for the Nations in Dallas. She lives in Bastrop with her husband and three children. Angela has written several short stories and books, including *the Toby the Trilby* series for kids. to find out more about her writing, go to
http://angelacastillowrites.weebly.com

Be sure to watch for *The River Girl's Christmas*, book 4 in the Texas Women of Spirit series, coming in August 2016.

Excerpt From
The River Girl's Song

Texas Women of Spirit
Book 1, Available on Amazon in
paperback and Kindle.

http://www.amazon.com/The-River-Girls-Song-Spirit-ebook/dp/B00X32KBL0/ref=pd_rhf_gw_p_img_1?ie=UTF8&refRID=18DCQ0M4FSR2VYKTRJ15

1

Scarlet Sunset

"We need to sharpen these knives again." Zillia examined her potato in the light from the window. Peeling took so long with a dull blade, and Mama had been extra fond of mash this month.

Mama poured cream up to the churn's fill line and slid the top over the dasher. "Yes, so many things to do! And we'll be even busier in a few weeks." She began to churn the butter, her arms stretched out to avoid her swollen belly. "Don't fret. Everything will settle into place."

"Tell that to Jeb when he comes in, hollering for his dinner," muttered Zillia. The potato turned into tiny bits beneath her knife.

"Don't be disrespectful." Though Mama spoke sharply, her mouth quirked up into a smile. She leaned over to examine Zillia's work. "Watch your fingers."

"Sorry, I wasn't paying attention." Zillia scooped the potato bits into the kettle and pulled another one out of the bag. Her long, slender fingers already bore several scars reaped by impatience.

"Ooh, someone's kicking pretty hard today." Mama rubbed her stomach.

Zillia looked away. When Papa was alive, she would have given anything for a little brother or sister. In the good times, the farm had prospered and she chose new shoes from a catalogue every year. Ice was delivered in the summer and firewood came in two loads at the beginning of winter. Back then, Mama could have hired a maid to help out when the little one came.

She and Mama spent most of their time working together, and they discussed everything. But she didn't dare talk about those days. Mama always cried.

"I might need you to finish this." Mama stopped for a moment and wiped her face with her muslin apron. "I'm feeling a little dizzy."

"Why don't you sit down and I'll make you some tea?" Zillia put down her knife and went to wash her hands in the basin.

Water, streaked with red, gushed from beneath Mama's petticoats. She gasped, stepped back and stared at the growing puddle on the floor. "Oh dear. I'm guessing it's time."

"Are you sure? Dr. Madison said you had weeks to go." Zillia had helped with plenty of births on the farm, but only for animals. From what she'd gathered, human babies brought far more fuss and trouble. She shook the water off her hands and went to her mother's side.

Mama sagged against Zillia's shoulder, almost throwing her off balance. She moaned and trembled. The wide eyes staring into Zillia's did not seem like they could belong to the prim, calm woman who wore a lace collar at all times, even while milking the goats.

Zillia steadied herself with one hand on the kitchen table. "We need to get you to a comfortable place. Does it hurt terribly?"

Mama's face relaxed and she stood a little straighter. "Sixteen years have passed since I went through this with you, but I remember." She wiped her eyes. "We have a while to go, don't be frightened. Just go tell your stepfather to fetch the doctor."

Zillia frowned, the way she always did when anyone referred to the man her mother married as her stepfather. Jeb had not been her choice, and was no kin to her. "Let me help you into bed first."

They moved in slow, shaky steps through the kitchen and into Mama's bedroom. Zillia hoped Mama couldn't feel her frenzied heartbeat. *I have no right to be afraid; it's not me who has to bring an entire baby into this world.*

Red stains crept up the calico hem of Mama's skirts as they dragged on the floor.

A sourness rose in the back of Zillia's throat. *This can't be right.* "Is it supposed to be such a mess?"

"Oh yes." Mama gave a weak chuckle. "And much more to come. Wait until you meet the new little one. It's always worth the trouble."

Mama grasped her arm when they reached the large bed, covered in a cheery blue and white quilt. "Before you go, help me get this dress off. Please?"

Zillia's hands shook so much she could hardly unfasten the buttons. It seemed like hours before she was able to get all forty undone, from Mama's lower back to the nape of her neck. She peeled the dress off the quivering shoulders, undoing the stays and laces until only the thin lace slip was left.

Another spasm ran through Mama's body. She hunched over and took several deep breaths. After a moment, she collected herself and stumbled out of the pile of clothing.

When Zillia gathered the dress to the side, she found a larger pool of blood under the cloth. Thin streams ran across the wood to meet the sunlight waning through the window panes. "There's so much blood, Mama, how can we make it stop?"

"Nothing can stop a baby coming. We just have to do the best we can and pray God will see us through." "I know, Mama, but can't you see... I don't know what to do." Zillia rubbed her temples and stepped back.

Mama's mouth was drawn and she stared past Zillia, like she wasn't there.

Mama won't want the bed ruined. Zillia pulled the quilt off the feather tick and set it aside. A stack of cloths were stored beneath the wash basin in preparation for this day. She spread them out over the mattress and helped her mother roll onto the bed.

Thin blue veins stood out on Mama's forehead. She squeezed her eyes shut. "Go out and find Jeb, like I told you. Then get some water boiling and come back in here as fast as you can."

Zillia grabbed her sunbonnet and headed out the door. "God, please, please let him be close. And please make him listen to me," she said aloud, like she usually prayed.

Parts of her doubted the Almighty God cared to read her thoughts, so she'd speak prayers when no one else could hear. At times she worried some busybody would find out and be scandalized by her lack of faith, but unless they could read thoughts, how would they know?

None of the urgency and fear enclosed in the house had seeped into the outside world. Serene pine trees, like teeth on a broken comb, lined the bluff leading to the Colorado River. Before her, stalks littered the freshly harvested cornfield, stretching into the distance. Chickens scattered as she rushed across the sun-baked earth, and goats bounded to the fence, sharp eyes watching for treats.

"Let Jeb be close!" she prayed again, clutching her sunbonnet strings in both fists. She hurried to the barn. Her mother's husband had spent the last few days repairing the goat fence, since the little rascals always found ways to escape. But he'd wanted to check over the back field today.

Sounds of iron striking wood came from inside. She released the breath she'd been holding and stepped into the gloomy barn.

Jeb's back was towards her, his shirt soaked through. Late summer afternoon. A terrible time for chores in Texas, and the worst time to be swollen with child, Mama said.

"Jeb, Mama says it's time. Please go get the doctor."

"Wha-at?" Jeb snarled. He always snarled when her mother wasn't around. He swung the axe hard into a log so it bit deep and stuck. The man turned and wiped the sweat from his thin, red face. Brown snakes of hair hung down to his shoulders in unkempt strands. "I got a whole day of work left and here it is, almost sunset. I don't have time to ride into town for that woman's fits and vapors. She ain't due yet."

Zillia fought for a reply. She couldn't go for the doctor herself; she'd never leave Mama alone.

Jeb reached for the axe.

"There's blood all over the floor. She says it's time, so it's time." Zillia tried to speak with authority, like Mama when she wanted to get a point across. "You need to go Jeb. Get going now."

When it came to farm work, Jeb moved like molasses. But the slap came so fast Zillia had no time to duck or defend herself. She fell to the ground and held her face. Skin burned under her fingers.

"Please, Jeb, please go for help!" she pleaded. Though he'd threatened her before, he'd never struck her.

"Shut up!" Jeb growled. "I'll go where and when I wish. No girl's gonna tell me what to do." He moved away, and she heard the horse nicker as he entered the stable.

Wooden walls swirled around Zillia's head. The anger and fear that coursed through her system overcame the pain and she pushed herself up and stood just in time to see Jeb riding down the road in the direction of the farm belonging to their closest neighbors, the Eckhart family.

They can get here faster than the doctor. First common sense thing the man's done all day. "Please God," she prayed again. "Please let Grandma Louise and Soonie be home."

###

Blood, scarlet like the garnets on Mama's first wedding ring, seemed to cover everything. The wooden floor slats. Linen sheets, brought in a trunk when their family came from Virginia. Zillia's fingers, all white and stained with the same sticky blood, holding Mama's as though they belonged to one hand.

The stench filled the room, sending invisible alarms to her brain. Throughout the birth, they had played in her head. *This can't be right. This can't be right.*\

The little mite had given them quite a tug of war, every bit as difficult as the goats when they twinned. Finally he'd come, covered in slippery blood that also gushed around him.

Over in a cradle given to them by a woman from church, the baby waved tiny fists in the air. His lips opened and his entire face became his mouth, in a mighty scream for one so small. Zillia had cleared his mouth and nose to make sure he could breath, wrapped him in a blanket, and gone back to her mother's side.

Mama's breaths came in ragged gasps. Her eyelids where closed but her eyes moved under the lids, as though she had the fever. Zillia pressed her mother's hand up to her own forehead, mindless of the smear of red it would leave behind.

The burned sun shrank behind the line of trees. No fire or lantern had been lit to stave off the darkness, but Zillia was too weary to care. Her spirits sank as her grasp on Mama's hand tightened.

At some point Mama's screams had turned into little moans and sobs, and mutterings Zillia couldn't understand. How long had it been since they'd spoken? The only clock in the house was on the kitchen mantle, but by the light Zillia figured an hour or more had passed since Jeb left. When the bloody tide had ebbed at last, Zillia wasn't sure if the danger was over, or if her mother simply didn't have more to bleed.

A knock came at the door. The sound she had waited and prayed for, what seemed like all her life. "Please come in." The words came in hoarse sections, as though she had to remind herself how to speak.

The door squeaked open and cool evening air blew through the room, a blessed tinge of relief from the stifling heat.

"Zillia, are you in here?" A tall, tan girl stepped into the room, carrying a lantern. Her golden-brown eyes darted from the mess, to the bed, to the baby in the cradle. "Oh, Zillia, Jeb met Grandma and me in town and told us to come. I thought Mrs. Bowen had weeks to go, yet." She set the light on the bedside table and rushed over to check the baby, her moccasins padding on the wooden floor.

"No doctor, Soonie?" Zillia croaked.

"Doctor Madison was delivering a baby across the river, and something's holding up the ferry. We passed Jeb at the dock, that's when he told us what was going on. The horses couldn't move any faster. I thought Grandma was going to unhitch the mare and ride bareback to get here."

In spite of the situation, Zillia's face cracked into a smile at the thought of tiny, stout Grandma Louise galloping in from town.

An old woman stepped in behind Soonie. Though Grandma Louise wasn't related to Zillia by blood, close friends called her 'grandma' anyway. She set down a bundle of blankets. A wrinkled hand went to her mouth while she surveyed the room, but when she caught Zillia's eye she gave a capable smile. "I gathered everything I could find from around the house and pulled the pot from the fire so we could get this little one cleaned up." She bustled over to the bedside. "Zillia, why don't you go in the kitchen and fill a washtub with warm water?"

Though Zillia heard the words, she didn't move. She might never stir again. For eternity she would stay in this place, willing her mother to keep breathing.

"Come on, girl." Grandma Louise tugged her arm, then stopped when she saw the pile of stained sheets. Her faded blue eyes watered.

Zillia blinked. "Mama, we have help." *Maybe everything will be all right.*

Grandma Louise had attended births for years before a doctor had come to Bastrop. She tried to pull Zillia's hand away from her mother's, but her fingers stuck.

Mama's eyes fluttered. "Zillia, my sweet girl. Where is my baby? Is he all right?"

Soonie gathered the tiny bundle in her arms and brought him over. "He's a pretty one, Mrs. Bowen. Ten fingers and toes, and looks healthy."

A smile tugged at one corner of Mama's pale lips. "He is pink and plump. Couldn't wish for more."

Grandma Louise came and touched Mama's forehead. "We're here now, Marjorie."

Mama's chest rose, and her exhaled breath rattled in her throat. Her eyes never left Zillia's face. "You'll do fine. Just fine. Don't—" She gasped once more, and her eyes closed.

Zillia had to lean forward to catch the words.

"Don't tell Jeb about the trunk."

"Mama?" Zillia grabbed the hand once more, but the strength had already left her mother's fingers. She tugged at her mother's arm, but it dropped back, limp on the quilt.

A tear trickled down Grandma Louise's wrinkled cheek. "Go on to the kitchen, Zillia. The baby should be nearer to the fire with this night air comin' on. Soonie and I will clean up in here."

"I don't want to leave her," Zillia protested. But one glance at her mother's face and the world seemed to collapse around her, like the woodpile when she didn't stack it right.

How could Mama slip away? A few hours ago they'd been laughing while the hens chased a grasshopper through the yard. They'd never spent a night apart and now Mama had left for another world all together. She pulled her hand back and stood to her feet. She blinked, wondering what had caused her to make such a motion.

Soonie held the baby out. His eyes, squinted shut from crying, opened for a moment and she caught a hint of blue. Blue like Mama's.

Zillia took him in her arms. Her half brother was heavier then he looked, and so warm. She tucked the cloth more tightly around him while he squirmed to get free. "I have to give him a bath." Red fingerprints dotted the blanket. "I need to wash my hands."

"Of course you do. Let's go see if the water is heated and we'll get you both cleaned up." Tears brimmed in Soonie's eyes and her lip trembled, but she picked the bundle of cloths that Grandma Louise had gathered and led the way into the kitchen, her smooth, black braid swinging to her waist as she walked.

Zillia cradled the baby in one arm, and her other hand strayed to her tangled mess of hair that had started the day as a tidy bun with ringlets in the front. What would Mama say? She stopped short while Soonie checked the water and searched for a washtub. *Mama will never say anything. Ever again.*

The baby began to wail again, louder this time, and her gulping sobs fell down to meet his.

Zillia sank to the floor, where she and the baby cried together until the bath had been prepared.

As Soonie wrapped the clean baby in a fresh blanket, Jeb burst into the house. He leaned against the door. "The doctor's on his way." His eyes widened when he saw the baby. "That's it, then? Boy or girl?"

"Boy." Soonie rose to her feet. "Jeb, where have you been? I saw you send someone else across on the ferry."

Jeb licked his lips and stared down at the floor. "Well, ah, I got word to the doctor. I felt a little thirsty, thought I'd celebrate. I mean, birthing is women's work, right?"

The bedroom door creaked open, and Grandma Louise stepped into the kitchen. Strands of gray hair had escaped her simple arrangement. Her eyes sparked in a way Zillia had only witnessed a few times, and knew shouldn't be taken lightly.

"Your thirst has cost you dearly, Jeb Bowen." Grandma Louise's Swedish accent grew heavier, as it always did with strong emotion. "While you drank the Devil's brew, your wife bled out her last hours. You could have spared a moment to bid her farewell. After all, she died to bring your child into the world."

Jeb stepped closer to Grandma Louise, and his lips twitched. Zillia knew he fought to hold back the spew of foul words she and her mother had been subjected to many times. Whether from shock or some distant respect for the elderly woman, he managed to keep silent while he pushed past Grandma Louise and into the bedroom.

Zillia stepped in behind him. Somehow, in the last quarter of an hour, Grandma Louise had managed to scrub away the worst of the blood and dispose of the stained sheets and petticoats. The blue quilt was smoothed over her mother's body, almost to her chin. Her hands where folded over her chest, like she always held them in church during prayer.

Tears threatened to spill out, but Zillia held them back. She wouldn't cry in front of Jeb.

The man reached over and touched Mama's cheek, smoothing a golden curl back into place above her forehead. "You was a good woman, Marjorie," he muttered.

"Jeb." Zillia stretched out her hand, but she didn't dare to touch him.

When he turned, his jaws were slack, and his eyes had lost their normal fire. "You stupid girl. Couldn't even save her."

Zillia flinched. A blow would have been better. *Surely the man isn't completely addled? Not even the doctor could have helped Mama.* She shrank back against the wall, and swallowed words dangerous to her own self.

Jeb stared at her for another moment, then bowed his head. "I guess that's that." He turned on his boot and walked out of the room.

Find out more about this book, and Angela Castillo's

other writings, at http://angelacastillowrites.weebly.com

Made in the USA
Charleston, SC
01 April 2016